This book was prepared
for the partially seeing by
<u>NATIONAL</u> <u>ASSOCIATION</u>
<u>FOR</u> <u>VISUALLY</u> <u>HANDICAPPED</u>
(A non-profit voluntary health agency)

3201 Balboa Street
San Francisco
California
94121

This book was prepared
for the

NATIONAL ASSOCIATION
for
VISUALLY HANDICAPPED

ISBN 0-89064-043-2

L O R D   O F   T H E   F L I E S

by

William Golding

VOLUME 1

Transcribed into large print
with the kind permission
of the publisher
G. P. PUTNAM'S SONS
(Copyright, 1954, 1955)

C δ ζ C

LORD OF THE FLIES

VOLUME 1

CONTENTS

The Sound of the Shell.................... 5

Fire on the Mountain.................... 58

Huts on the Beach.................... 93

Painted Faces and Long Hair........... 115

Beast from Water...................... 153

Beast from Air........................ 195

CHAPTER ONE

THE SOUND OF THE SHELL

The boy with fair hair lowered himself down the last few feet of rock and began to pick his way toward the lagoon. Though he had taken off his school sweater and trailed it now from one hand, his grey shirt stuck to him and his hair was plastered to his forehead. All round him the long scar smashed into the jungle was a bath of heat. He was clambering heavily among the creepers and broken trunks when a bird, a vision of red and yellow, flashed upwards with a witch-like cry; and this cry was echoed by another.

"Hi!" it said. "Wait a minute!"

The undergrowth at the side of the scar was shaken and a multitude of raindrops fell pattering.

"Wait a minute," the voice said. "I got caught up."

The fair boy stopped and jerked his stockings with an automatic gesture that made

the jungle seem for a moment like the Home
Counties.

The voice spoke again.

"I can't hardly move with all these creeper
things."

The owner of the voice came backing out of
the undergrowth so that twigs scratched on
a greasy wind-breaker. The naked crooks of
his knees were plump, caught and scratched
by thorns. He bent down, removed the
thorns carefully, and turned round. He was
shorter than the fair boy and very fat. He
came forward, searching out safe lodgements
for his feet, and then looked up through
thick spectacles.

"Where's the man with the megaphone?"

The fair boy shook his head.

"This is an island. At least I think it's
an island. That's a reef out in the sea.
Perhaps there aren't any grown-ups anywhere."

The fat boy looked startled.

"There was that pilot. But he wasn't in the passenger cabin, he was up in front."

The fair boy was peering at the reef through screwed-up eyes.

"All them other kids," the fat boy went on. "Some of them must have got out. They must have, mustn't they?"

The fair boy began to pick his way as casually as possible toward the water. He tried to be offhand and not too obviously unin- terested, but the fat boy hurried after him.

"Aren't there any grownups at all?"

"I don't think so."

The fair boy said this solemnly; but then the delight of a realized ambition overcame him. In the middle of the scar he stood on his head and grinned at the reversed fat boy.

"No grownups!"

The fat boy thought for a moment.

"That pilot."

The fair boy allowed his feet to come down and sat on the steamy earth.

"He must have flown off after he dropped us. He couldn't land here. Not in a plane with wheels."

"We was attacked!"

"He'll be back all right."

The fat boy shook his head.

"When we was coming down I looked through one of them windows. I saw the other part of the plane. There were flames coming out of it."

He looked up and down the scar.

"And this is what the cabin done."

The fair boy reached out and touched the jagged end of a trunk. For a moment he looked interested.

"What happened to it?" he asked. "Where's it got to now?"

"That storm dragged it out to sea. It wasn't half dangerous with all them tree trunks falling. There must have been some kids still in it."

He hesitated for a moment, then spoke again.

"What's your name?"

"Ralph."

The fat boy waited to be asked his name in turn but this proffer of acquaintance was not made; the fair boy called Ralph smiled vaguely, stood up, and began to make his way once more toward the lagoon. The fat boy hung steadily at his shoulder.

"I expect there's a lot more of us scattered about. You haven't seen any others, have you?"

Ralph shook his head and increased his speed. Then he tripped over a branch and came down with a crash.

The fat boy stood by him, breathing hard.

"My auntie told me not to run," he explained, "on account of my asthma."

"Ass-mar?"

"That's right. Can't catch me breath. I was the only boy in our school what had asthma," said the fat boy with a touch of pride. "And I've been wearing specs since I was three."

He took off his glasses and held them out to Ralph, blinking and smiling, and then started to wipe them against his grubby wind-breaker. An expression of pain and inward concentration altered the pale contours of his face. He smeared the sweat from his cheeks and quickly adjusted the spectacles on his nose.

"Them fruit."

He glanced round the scar.

"Them fruit," he said, "I expect--"

He put on his glasses, waded away from Ralph,
and crouched down among the tangled foliage.

"I'll be out again in just a minute--"

Ralph disentangled himself cautiously and
stole away through the branches. In a few
seconds the fat boy's grunts were behind
him and he was hurrying toward the screen
that still lay between him and the lagoon.
He climbed over a broken trunk and was out
of the jungle.

The shore was fledged with palm trees.
These stood or leaned or reclined against
the light and their green feathers were a
hundred feet up in the air. The ground beneath them was a bank covered with coarse
grass, torn everywhere by the upheavals of
fallen trees, scattered with decaying coconuts and palm saplings. Behind this was the
darkness of the scar. Ralph stood, one hand
against a grey trunk, and screwed up his
eyes against the shimmering water. Out
there perhaps a mile away, the white surf
flinked on a coral reef, and beyond that the
open sea was dark blue. Within the irregular

arc of coral the lagoon was still as a
mountain lake--blue of all shades and shadowy
green and purple. The beach between the
palm terrace and the water was a thin stick,
endless apparently, for to Ralph's left the
perspectives of palm and beach and water
drew to a point at infinity; and always,
almost visible, was the heat.

He jumped down from the terrace. The sand
was thick over his black shoes and the heat
hit him. He became conscious of the weight
of clothes, kicked his shoes off fiercely
and ripped off each stocking with its elastic garter in a single movement. Then he
leapt back on the terrace, pulled off his
shirt, and stood there among the skull-like
coconuts with green shadows from the palms
and the forest sliding over his skin. He
undid the snake-clasp of his belt, lugged
off his shorts and pants, and stood there
naked, looking at the dazzling beach and the
water.

He was old enough, twelve years and a few
months, to have lost the prominent tummy
of childhood; and not yet old enough for
adolescence to have made him awkward. You

could see now that he might make a boxer,
as far as width and heaviness of shoulders
went, but there was a mildness about his
mouth and eyes that proclaimed no devil. He
patted the palm trunk softly, and, forced
at last to believe in the reality of the
island, laughed delightedly again and stood
on his head. He turned neatly on to his
feet, jumped down to the beach, knelt and
swept a double armful of sand into a pile
against his chest. Then he sat back and
looked at the water with bright, excited
eyes.

"Ralph--"

The fat boy lowered himself over the terrace
and sat down carefully, using the edge as
a seat.

"I'm sorry I been such a time. Them fruit--"

He wiped his glasses and adjusted them on
his button nose. The frame had made a deep,
pink "V" on the bridge. He looked criti-
cally at Ralph's golden body and then down
at his clothes. He laid a hand on the end
of a zipper that extended down his chest.

"My auntie--"

Then he opened the zipper with decision and pulled the whole wind-breaker over his head.

"There!"

Ralph looked at him sidelong and said noth-ing. "I expect we'll want to know all their names," said the fat boy,"and make a list. We ought to have a meeting."

Ralph did not take the hint so the fat boy was forced to continue.

"I don't care what they call me," he said confidentially, "so long as they don't call me what they used to call me at school."

Ralph was faintly interested.

"What was that?"

The fat boy glanced over his shoulder, then leaned toward Ralph.

He whispered.

"They used to call me 'Piggy.'"

Ralph shrieked with laughter. He jumped up.

"Piggy! Piggy!"

"Ralph--please!"

Piggy clasped his hands in apprehension.

"I said I didn't want--"

"Piggy! Piggy!"

Ralph danced out into the hot air of the
beach and then returned as a fighter-plane
with wings swept back, and machine-gunned
Piggy.

"Sche-aa-ow!"

He dived in the sand at Piggy's feet and
lay there laughing.

"Piggy!"

Piggy grinned reluctantly, pleased despite
himself at even this much recognition.

"So long as you don't tell the others--"

Ralph giggled into the sand. The expression of pain and concentration returned to Piggy's face.

"Half a sec'."

He hastened back into the forest. Ralph stood up and trotted along to the right.

Here the beach was interrupted abruptly by the square motif of the landscape; a great platform of pink granite thrust up uncompromisingly through forest and terrace and sand and lagoon to make a raised jetty four feet high. The top of this was covered with a thin layer of soil and coarse grass and shaded with young palm trees. There was not enough soil for them to grow to any height and when they reached perhaps twenty feet they fell and dried, forming a criss-cross pattern of trunks, very convenient to sit on. The palms that still stood made a green roof, covered on the underside with a quivering tangle of reflections from the lagoon. Ralph hauled himself onto this platform, noted the coolness and shade, shut one eye,

and decided that the shadows on his body
were really green. He picked his way to the
seaward edge of the platform and stood looking down into the water. It was clear to
the bottom and bright with the efflorescence
of tropical weed and coral. A school of
tiny, glittering fish flicked hither and
thither. Ralph spoke to himself, sounding
the bass strings of delight.

"Whizzoh!"

Beyond the platform there was more enchant-
ment. Some act of God--a typhoon perhaps,
or the storm that had accompanied his own
arrival--had banked sand inside the lagoon
so that there was a long, deep pool in the
beach with a high ledge of pink granite at
the further end. Ralph had been deceived
before now by the specious appearance of
depth in a beach pool and he approached this
one preparing to be disappointed. But the
island ran true to form and the incredible
pool, which clearly was only invaded by the
sea at high tide, was so deep at one end as
to be dark green. Ralph inspected the whole
thirty yards carefully and then plunged in.
The water was warmer than his blood and he
might have been swimming in a huge bath.

Piggy appeared again, sat on the rocky
ledge, and watched Ralph's green and white
body enviously.

"You can't half swim."

"Piggy."

Piggy took off his shoes and socks, ranged
them carefully on the ledge, and tested
the water with one toe.

"It's hot!"

"What did you expect?"

"I didn't expect nothing. My auntie--"

"Sucks to your auntie!"

Ralph did a surface dive and swam under
water with his eyes open; the sandy edge
of the pool loomed up like a hillside. He
turned over, holding his nose, and a golden
light danced and shattered just over his
face. Piggy was looking determined and
began to take off his shorts. Presently
he was palely and fatly naked. He tiptoed

down the sandy side of the pool, and sat
there up to his neck in water smiling
proudly at Ralph.

"Aren't you going to swim?"

Piggy shook his head.

"I can't swim. I wasn't allowed. My
asthma--"

"Sucks to your ass-mar!"

Piggy bore this with a sort of humble pa-
tience.

"You can't half swim well."

Ralph paddled backwards down the slope,
immersed his mouth and blew a jet of water
into the air. Then he lifted his chin and
spoke.

"I could swim when I was five. Daddy taught
me. He's a commander in the Navy. When he
gets leave he'll come and rescue us. What's
your father?"

Piggy flushed suddenly.

"My dad's dead," he said quickly, "and my mum--"

He took off his glasses and looked vainly for something with which to clean them.

"I used to live with my auntie. She kept a candy store. I used to get ever so many candies. As many as I liked. When'll your dad rescue us?"

"Soon as he can."

Piggy rose dripping from the water and stood naked, cleaning his glasses with a sock. The only sound that reached them now through the heat of the morning was the long, grinding roar of the breakers on the reef.

"How does he know we're here?"

Ralph lolled in the water. Sleep enveloped him like the swathing mirages that were wresting with the brilliance of the lagoon.

"How does he know we're here?"

Because, thought Ralph, because, because.
The roar from the reef became very distant.

"They'd tell him at the airport."

Piggy shook his head, put on his flashing
glasses and looked down at Ralph.

"Not them. Didn't you hear what the pilot
said? About the atom bomb? They're all
dead."

Ralph pulled himself out of the water, stood
facing Piggy, and considered this unusual
problem.

Piggy persisted.

"This an island, isn't it?"

"I climbed a rock," said Ralph slowly, "and
I think this is an island."

"They're all dead," said Piggy, "an' this
is an island. Nobody don't know we're here.
Your dad don't know, nobody don't know--"

His lips quivered and the spectacles were
dimmed with mist.

"We may stay here till we die."

With that word the heat seemed to increase till it became a threatening weight and the lagoon attacked them with a blinding effulgence.

"Get my clothes," muttered Ralph. "Along there."

He trotted through the sand, enduring the sun's enmity, crossed the platform and found his scattered clothes. To put on a grey shirt once more was strangely pleasing. Then he climbed the edge of the platform and sat in the green shade on a convenient trunk. Piggy hauled himself up, carrying most of his clothes under his arms. Then he sat carefully on a fallen trunk near the little cliff that fronted the lagoon; and the tangled reflections quivered over him.

Presently he spoke.

"We got to find the others. We got to do something."

Ralph said nothing. Here was a coral

island. Protected from the sun, ignoring
Piggy's ill-omened talk, he dreamed pleasantly.

Piggy insisted.

"How many of us are there?"

Ralph came forward and stood by Piggy.

"I don't know."

Here and there, little breezes crept over
the polished waters beneath the haze of
heat. When these breezes reached the
platform the palm fronds would whisper, so
that spots of blurred sunlight slid over
their bodies or moved like bright, winged
things in the shade.

Piggy looked up at Ralph. All the shadows
of Ralph's face were reversed; green above,
bright below from the lagoon. A blur of
sunlight was crawling across his hair.

"We got to do something."

Ralph looked through him. Here at last was
the imagined but never fully realized place

leaping into real life. Ralph's lips parted in a delighted smile and Piggy, taking this smile to himself as a mark of recognition, laughed with pleasure.

"If it really is an island--"

"What's that?"

Ralph had stopped smiling and was pointing into the lagoon. Something creamy lay among the ferny weeds.

"A stone."

"No. A shell."

Suddenly Piggy was a-bubble with decorous excitement.

"S'right. It's a shell! I seen one like that before. On someone's back wall. A conch he called it. He used to blow it and then his mum would come. It's ever so valuable--"

Near to Ralph's elbow a palm sapling leaned out over the lagoon. Indeed, the weight

was already pulling a lump from the poor
soil and soon it would fall. He tore out
the stem and began to poke about in the
water, while the brilliant fish flicked
away on this side and that. Piggy leaned
dangerously.

"Careful! You'll break it--"

"Shut up."

Ralph spoke absently. The shell was inter-
esting and pretty and a worthy plaything;
but the vivid phantoms of his day-dream
still interposed between him and Piggy, who
in this context was an irrelevance. The
palm sapling, bending, pushed the shell
across the weeds. Ralph used one hand as
a fulcrum and pressed down with the other
till the shell rose, dripping, and Piggy
could make a grab.

Now the shell was no longer a thing seen
but not to be touched, Ralph too became
excited. Piggy babbled:

"--a conch; ever so expensive. I bet if
you wanted to buy one, you'd have to pay

pounds and pounds and pounds--he had it on
his garden wall, and my auntie--"

Ralph took the shell from Piggy and a little
water ran down his arm. In color the shell
was deep cream, touched here and there with
fading pink. Between the point, worn away
into a little hole, and the pink lips of
the mouth, lay eighteen inches of shell with
a slight spiral twist and covered with a
delicate, embossed pattern. Ralph shook
sand out of the deep tube.

"--mooed like a cow," he said. "He had
some white stones too, an' a bird cage with
a green parrot. He didn't blow the white
stones, of course, an' he said--"

Piggy paused for breath and stroked the
glistening thing that lay in Ralph's hands.

"Ralph!"

Ralph looked up.

"We can use this to call the others. Have
a meeting. They'll come when they hear
us--"

He beamed at Ralph.

"That was what you meant, didn't you?
That's why you got the conch out of the
water?"

Ralph pushed back his fair hair.

"How did your friend blow the conch?"

"He kind of spat," said Piggy. "My auntie
wouldn't let me blow on account of my
asthma. He said you blew from down here."
Piggy laid a hand on his jutting abdomen.
"You try, Ralph. You'll call the others."

Doubtfully, Ralph laid the small end of
the shell against his mouth and blew. There
came a rushing sound from its mouth but
nothing more. Ralph wiped the salt water
off his lips and tried again, but the shell
remained silent.

"He kind of spat."

Ralph pursed his lips and squirted air into
the shell, which emitted a low, farting
noise. This amused both boys so much that

Ralph went on squirting for some minutes,
between bouts of laughter.

"He blew from down here."

Ralph grasped the idea and hit the shell
with air from his diaphragm. Immediately
the thing sounded. A deep, harsh note
boomed under the palms, spread through the
intricacies of the forest and echoed back
from the pink granite of the mountain.
Clouds of birds rose from the treetops, and
something squealed and ran in the undergrowth.

Ralph took the shell away from his lips.

"Gosh!"

His ordinary voice sounded like a whisper
after the harsh note of the conch. He laid
the conch against his lips, took a deep
breath and blew once more. The note boomed
again: and then at his firmer pressure, the
note, fluking up an octave, became a stri-
dent blare more penetrating than before.
Piggy was shouting something, his face
pleased, his glasses flashing. The birds

cried, small animals scuttered. Ralph's
breath failed; the note dropped the octave,
became a low wubber, was a rush of air.

The conch was silent, a gleaming tusk;
Ralph's face was dark with breathlessness
and the air over the island was full of
bird-clamor and echoes ringing.

"I bet you can hear that for miles."

Ralph found his breath and blew a series of
short blasts.

Piggy exclaimed: "There's one!"

A child had appeared among the palms, about
a hundred yards along the beach. He was a
boy of perhaps six years, sturdy and fair,
his clothes torn, his face covered with a
sticky mess of fruit. His trousers had been
lowered for an obvious purpose and had only
been pulled back half-way. He jumped off
the palm terrace into the sand and his
trousers fell about his ankles; he stepped
out of them and trotted to the platform.
Piggy helped him up. Meanwhile Ralph continued to blow till voices shouted in the
forest. The small boy squatted in front of

Ralph, looking up brightly and vertically.
As he received the reassurance of something
purposeful being done he began to look satisfied, and his only clean digit, a pink
thumb, slid into his mouth.

Piggy leaned down to him.

"What's your name?"

"Johnny."

Piggy muttered the name to himself and then
shouted it to Ralph, who was not interested
because he was still blowing. His face was
dark with the violent pleasure of making
this stupendous noise, and his heart was
making the stretched shirt shake. The
shouting in the forest was nearer.

Signs of life were visible now on the beach.
The sand, trembling beneath the heat haze,
concealed many figures in its miles of
length; boys were making their way toward
the platform through the hot, dumb sand.
Three small children, no older than Johnny,
appeared from startlingly close at hand
where they had been gorging fruit in the

forest. A dark little boy, not much younger
than Piggy, parted a tangle of undergrowth,
walked on to the platform, and smiled cheer-
fully at everybody. More and more of them
came. Taking their cue from the innocent
Johnny, they sat down on the fallen palm
trunks and waited. Ralph continued to blow
short, penetrating blasts. Piggy moved
among the crowd, asking names and frowning
to remember them. The children gave him
the same simple obedience that they had
given to the men with megaphones. Some were
naked and carrying their clothes; others
half-naked, or more or less dressed, in
school uniforms, grey, blue, fawn, jacketed
or jerseyed. There were badges, motoes
even, stripes of color in stockings and
pullovers. Their heads clustered above the
trunks in the green shade; heads brown,
fair, black, chestnut, sandy, mouse-colored;
heads muttering, whispering, heads full of
eyes that watched Ralph and speculated.
Something was being done.

The children who came along the beach,
singly or in twos, leapt into visibility
when they crossed the line from heat haze
to nearer sand. Here, the eye was first

attracted to a black, bat-like creature that
danced on the sand, and only later perceived
the body above it. The bat was the child's
shadow, shrunk by the vertical sun to a
patch between the hurrying feet. Even while
he blew, Ralph noticed the last pair of
bodies that reached the platform above a
fluttering patch of black. The two boys,
bullet-headed and with hair like tow, flung
themselves down and lay grinning and panting
at Ralph like dogs. They were twins, and
the eye was shocked and incredulous at such
cheery duplication. They breathed together,
they grinned together, they were chunky and
vital. They raised wet lips at Ralph, for
they seemed provided with not quite enough
skin, so that their profiles were blurred
and their mouths pulled open. Piggy bent
his flashing glasses to them and could be
heard between the blasts, repeating their
names.

"Sam, Eric, Sam, Eric."

Then he got muddled; the twins shook their
heads and pointed at each other and the
crowd laughed.

At last Ralph ceased to blow and sat there,
the conch trailing from one hand, his head
bowed on his knees. As the echoes died
away so did the laughter, and there was
silence.

Within the diamond haze of the beach something dark was fumbling along. Ralph saw
it first, and watched till the intentness
of his gaze drew all eyes that way. Then
the creature stepped from mirage on to
clear sand, and they saw that the darkness
was not all shadows but mostly clothing.
The creature was a party of boys, marching
approximately in step in two parallel lines
and dressed in strangely eccentric clothing.
Shorts, shirts, and different garments they
carried in their hands; but each boy wore
a square black cap with a silver badge on
it. Their bodies, from throat to ankle,
were hidden by black cloaks which bore a
long silver cross on the left breast and
each neck was finished off with a hambone
frill. The heat of the tropics, the descent,
the search for food, and now this sweaty
march along the blazing beach had given
them the complexions of newly washed plums.
The boy who controlled them was dressed in

the same way though his cap badge was
golden. When his party was about ten yards
from the platform he shouted an order and
they halted, gasping, sweating, swaying in
the fierce light. The boy himself came
forward, vaulted on to the platform with his
cloak flying, and peered into what to him
was almost complete darkness.

"Where's the man with the trumpet?"

Ralph, sensing his sun-blindness, answered
him.

"There's no man with a trumpet. Only me."

The boy came close and peered down at Ralph,
screwing up his face as he did so. What he
saw of the fair-haired boy with the creamy
shell on his knees did not seem to satisfy
him. He turned quickly, his black cloak
circling.

"Isn't there a ship, then?"

Inside the floating cloak he was tall, thin,
and bony: and his hair was red beneath the
black cap. His face was crumpled and freckled, and ugly without silliness. Out of

this face stared two light blue eyes,
frustrated now, and turning, or ready to
turn, to anger.

"Isn't there a man here?"

Ralph spoke to his back.

"No. We're having a meeting. Come and
join in."

The group of cloaked boys began to scatter
from close line. The tall boy shouted at
them.

"Choir! Stand still!"

Wearily obedient, the choir huddled into
line and stood there swaying in the sun.
None the less, some began to protest
faintly.

"But Merridew. Please, Merridew . . .
can't we?"

Then one of the boys flopped on his face
in the sand and the line broke up. They
heaved the fallen boy to the platform and

let him lie. Merridew, his eyes staring, made the best of a bad job.

"All right then. Sit down. Let him alone."

"But Merridew."

"He's always throwing a faint," said Merridew. He did in Gib.; and Addis; and at matins over the precentor."

This last piece of shop brought sniggers from the choir, who perched like black birds on the criss-cross trunks and examined Ralph with interest. Piggy asked no names. He was intimidated by this uniformed superiority and the offhand authority in Merridew's voice. He shrank to the other side of Ralph and busied himself with his glasses.

Merridew turned to Ralph.

"Aren't there any grownups?"

"No."

Merridew sat down on a trunk and looked round the circle.

"Then we'll have to look after ourselves."

Secure on the other side of Ralph, Piggy
spoke timidly.

"That's why Ralph made a meeting. So as we
can decide what to do. We've heard names.
That's Johnny. Those two--they're twins,
Sam 'n Eric. Which is Eric--" You? No--
you're Sam--"

"I'm Sam--"

"'n I'm Eric."

"We'd better all have names," said Ralph,
"so I'm Ralph."

"Kids' names," said Merridew. "Why should
I be Jack? I'm Merridew."

Ralph turned to him quickly. This was the
voice of one who knew his own mind.

"Then," went on Piggy, "that boy--I for-
get--"

"You're talking too much," said Jack Merridew. "Shut up, Fatty."

Laughter arose.

"He's not Fatty," cried Ralph, "his real name's Piggy!"

"Piggy!"

"Piggy!"

"Oh, Piggy!"

A storm of laughter arose and even the tiniest child joined in. For the moment the boys were a closed circuit of sympathy with Piggy outside: he went very pink, bowed his head and cleaned his glasses again.

Finally the laughter died away and the naming continued. There was Maurice, next in size among the choir boys to Jack, but broad and grinning all the time. There was a slight, furtive boy whom no one knew, who kept to himself with an inner intensity of avoidance and secrecy. He muttered that his name was Roger and was silent again. Bill, Robert, Harold, Henry; the choir boy who had fainted sat up against a palm trunk,

smiled pallidly at Ralph and said that his
name was Simon.

Jack spoke.

"We've got to decide about being rescued."

There was a buzz. One of the small boys,
Henry, said that he wanted to go home.

"Shut up," said Ralph absently. He lifted
the conch. "Seems to me we ought to have a
chief to decide things."

"A chief! A chief!"

"I ought to be chief," said Jack with
simple arrogance, "because I'm chapter
chorister and head boy. I can sing C
sharp."

Another buzz.

"Well then, said Jack, "I--"

He hesitated. The dark boy, Roger, stirred
at last and spoke up.

"Let's have a vote."

"Yes!"

"Vote for chief!"

"Let's vote--"

This toy of voting was almost as pleasing
as the conch. Jack started to protest but
the clamor changed from the general wish
for a chief to an election by acclaim of
Ralph himself. None of the boys could have
found good reason for this; what intelligence had been shown was traceable to Piggy
while the most obvious leader was Jack.
But there was a stillness about Ralph as
he sat that marked him out: there was his
size, and attractive appearance; and most
obscurely, yet most powerfully, there was
the conch. The being that had blown that,
had sat waiting for them on the platform
with the delicate thing balanced on his
knees, was set apart.

"Him with the shell."

"Ralph! Ralph!"

"Let him be chief with the trumpet-thing."

Ralph raised a hand for silence.

"All right. Who wants Jack for chief?"

With dreary obedience the choir raised
their hands.

"Who wants me?"

Every hand outside the choir except Piggy's
was raised immediately. Then Piggy, too,
raised his hand grudgingly into the air.

Ralph counted.

"I'm chief then."

The circle of boys broke into applause.
Even the choir applauded; and the freckles
on Jack's face disappeared under a blush of
mortification. He started up, then changed
his mind and sat down again while the air
rang Ralph looked at him, eager to offer
something.

"The choir belongs to you, of course."

"They could be the army--"

"Or hunters--"

"They could be--"

The suffusion drained away from Jack's face.
Ralph waved again for silence.

"Jack's in charge of the choir. They can
be--what do you want them to be?"

"Hunters."

Jack and Ralph smiled at each other with
shy liking. The rest began to talk eagerly.

Jack stood up.

"All right, choir. Take off your togs."

As if released from class, the choir boys
stood up, chattered, piled their black
cloaks on the grass. Jack laid his on the
trunk by Ralph. His grey shorts were
sticking to him with sweat. Ralph glanced
at them admiringly, and when Jack saw his
glance he explained.

"I tried to get over that hill to see if

there was water all round. But your shell
called us."

Ralph smiled and held up the conch for
silence.

"Listen, everybody I've got to have time
to think things out. I can't decide what
to do straight off. If this isn't an
island we might be rescued straight away.
So we've got to decide if this is an
island. Everybody must stay round here
and wait and not go away. Three of us--
if we take more we'd get all mixed, and
lose each other--three of us will go on
an expedition and find out. I'll go, and
Jack, and, and. . . ."

He looked round the circle of eager faces.
There was no lack of boys to choose from.

"And Simon."

The boys round Simon giggled, and he stood
up, laughing a little. Now that the pallor
of his faint was over, he was a skinny,
vivid little boy, with a glance coming up
from under a hut of straight hair that hung
down, black and coarse.

He nodded at Ralph.

"I'll come."

"And I--"

Jack snatched from behind him a sizable sheath-knife and clouted it into a trunk. The buzz rose and died away.

Piggy stirred.

"I'll come."

Ralph turned to him.

"You're no good on a job like this."

"All the same--"

"We don't want you," said Jack, flatly. "Three's enough."

Piggy's glasses flashed.

"I was with him when he found the conch. I was with him before anyone else was."

Jack and the others paid no attention.
There was a general dispersal. Ralph, Jack
and Simon jumped off the platform and walked
along the sand past the bathing pool. Piggy
hung bumbling behind them.

"If Simon walks in the middle of us," said
Ralph, "then we could talk over his head."

The three of them fell into step. This
meant that every now and then Simon had to
do a double shuffle to catch up with the
others. Presently Ralph stopped and turned
back to Piggy.

"Look,"

Jack and Simon pretended to notice nothing.
They walked on.

"You can't come."

Piggy's glasses were misted again--this
time with humiliation.

"You told 'em. After what I said."

His face flushed, his mouth trembled.

"After I said I didn't want--"

"What on earth are you talking about?"

"About being called Piggy. I said I didn't care as long as they didn't call me Piggy; an' I said not to tell and then you went an' said straight out--"

Stillness descended on them. Ralph, looking with more understanding at Piggy, saw that he was hurt and crushed. He hovered between the two courses of apology or further insult.

"Better Piggy than Fatty," he said at last, with the directness of genuine leadership, "and anyway, I'm sorry if you feel like that. Now go back, Piggy, and take names. That's your job. So long."

He turned and raced after the other two. Piggy stood and the rose of indignation faded slowly from his cheeks. He went back to the platform.

The three boys walked briskly on the sand. The tide was low and there was a strip of weed-strewn beach that was almost as firm

as a road. A kind of glamour was spread
over them and the scene and they were
conscious of the glamour and made happy by
it. They turned to each other, laughing
excitedly, talking, not listening. The air
was bright. Ralph, faced by the task of
translating all this into an explanation,
stood on his head and fell over. When they
had done laughing, Simon stroked Ralph's
arm shyly; and they had to laugh again.

"Come on," said Jack presently, "we're
explorers."

"We'll go to the end of the island," said
Ralph, "and look round the corner.

"If it is an island--"

Now, toward the end of the afternoon, the
mirages were settling a little. They found
the end of the island, quite distinct, and
not magicked out of shape or sense. There
was a jumble of the usual squareness, with
one great block sitting out in the lagoon.
Sea birds were nesting there.

"Like icing," said Ralph, "on a pink cake."

"We shan't see round this corner," said
Jack, "because there isn't one. Only a
slow curve--and you can see, the rocks get
worse--"

Ralph shaded his eyes and followed the
jagged outline of the crags up toward the
mountain. This part of the beach was nearer
the mountain than any other that they had
seen.

"We'll try climbing the mountain from here,"
he said. "I should think this is the easi-
est way. There's less of that jungly stuff;
and more pink rock. Come on."

The three boys began to scramble up. Some
unknown force had wrenched and shattered
these cubes so that they lay askew, often
piled diminishingly on each other. The
most usual feature of the rock was a pink
cliff surmounted by a skewed block; and
that again surmounted, and that again, till
the pinkness became a stack of balanced
rock projecting through the looped fantasy
of the forest creepers. Where the pink
cliffs rose out of the ground there were
often narrow tracks winding upwards. They

could edge along them, deep in the plant
world, their faces to the rock.

"What made this track?"

Jack paused, wiping the sweat from his
face. Ralph stood by him, breathless.

"Men?"

Jack shook his head.

"Animals."

Ralph peered into the darkness under the
trees. The forest minutely vibrated.

"Come on."

The difficulty was not the steep ascent
round the shoulders of rock, but the occasional plunges through the undergrowth
to get to the next path. Here the roots
and stems of creepers were in such tangles
that the boys had to thread through them
like pliant needles. Their only guide,
apart from the brown ground and occasional
flashes of light through the foliage, was

the tendency of slope; whether this hole, laced as it was with the cables of creeper, stood higher than that.

Somehow, they moved up.

Immured in these tangles, at perhaps their most difficult moment, Ralph turned with shining eyes to the others.

"Wacco."

"Wizard."

"Smashing."

The cause of their pleasure was not obvious. All three were hot, dirty and exhausted. Ralph was badly scratched. The creepers were as thick as their thighs and left little but tunnels for further penetration. Ralph shouted experimentally and they lis- tened to the muted echoes.

"This is real exploring," said Jack "I bet nobody's been here before."

"We ought to draw a map," said Ralph, "only we haven't any paper."

"We could make scratches on bark," said
Simon, "and rub black stuff in."

Again came the solemn communion of shining
eyes in the gloom.

"Wacco."

"Wizard"

There was no place for standing on one's
head. This time Ralph expressed the intensity of his emotion by pretending to knock
Simon down; and soon they were a happy,
heaving pile in the under-dusk.

When they had fallen apart Ralph spoke
first.

"Got to get on."

The pink granite of the next cliff was
further back from the creepers and trees
so that they could trot up the path. This
again led into more open forest so that
they had a glimpse of the spread sea. With
openness came the sun; it dried the sweat
that had soaked their clothes in the dark,

damp heat. At last the way to the top
looked like a scramble over pink rock, with
no more plunging through darkness. The
boys chose their way through defiles and
over heaps of sharp stone.

"look! Look!"

High over this end of the island, the shattered rocks lifted up their stacks and
chimneys. This one, against which Jack
leaned, moved with a grating sound when
they pushed.

"Come on--"

But not "Come on" to the top. The assault
on the summit must wait while the three
boys accepted this challenge. The rock
was as large as a small motor car.

"Heave!"

Sway back and forth, catch the rhythm.

"Heave!"

Increase the swing of the pendulum, increase, increase, come up and bear against

that point of furthest balance--increase--
increase--

"Heave!"

The great rock loitered, poised on one toe,
decided not to return, moved through the
air, fell, struck, turned over, leapt
droning through the air and smashed a deep
hole in the canopy of the forest. Echoes
and birds flew, white and pink dust floated,
the forest further down shook as with the
passage of an enraged monster: and then the
island was still.

"Wacco!"

"Like a bomb!"

"Whee-aa-oo!"

Not for five minutes could they drag themselves away from this triumph. But they
left at last.

The way to the top was easy after that.
As they reached the last stretch Ralph
stopped.

"Golly!"

They were on the lip of a circular hollow
in the side of the mountain. This was
filled with a blue flower, a rock plant of
some sort, and the overflow hung down the
vent and spilled lavishly among the canopy
of the forest. The air was thick with
butterflies, lifting, fluttering, settling.

Beyond the hollow was the square top of the
mountain and soon they were standing on it.

They had guessed before that this was an
island: clambering among the pink rocks,
with the sea on either side, and the crystal
heights of air, they had known by some in-
stinct that the sea lay on every side. But
there seemed something more fitting in
leaving the last word till they stood on
the top, and could see a circular horizon
of water.

Ralph turned to the others.

"This belongs to us."

It was roughly boat-shaped: humped near thij
end with behind them the jumbled descent to

the shore. On either side rocks, cliffs,
treetops and a steep slope: forward there,
the length of the boat, a tamer descent,
tree-clad, with hints of pink: and then
the jungly flat of the island, dense green,
but drawn at the end to a pink tail. There,
where the island petered out in water, was
another island; a rock, almost detached,
standing like a fort, facing them across
the green with one bold, pink bastion.

The boys surveyed all this, then looked out
to sea. They were high up and the afternoon
had advanced; the view was not robbed of
sharpness by mirage.

"That's a reef. A coral reef. I've seen
pictures like that."

The reef enclosed more than one side of the
island, lying perhaps a mile out and parallel to what they now thought of as their
beach. The coral was scribbled in the sea
as though a giant had bent down to reproduce
the shape of the island in a flowing chalk
line but tired before he had finished. Inside was peacock water, rocks and weed
showing as in an aquarium; outside was the

dark blue of the sea. The tide was running
so that long streaks of foam tailed away
from the reef and for a moment they felt
that the boat was moving steadily astern.

Jack pointed down.

"That's where we landed."

Beyond falls and cliffs there was a gash
visible in the trees; there were the splin-
tered trunks and then the drag, leaving
only a fringe of palm between the scar and
the sea. There, too, jutting into the lagoon, was the platform, with insect-like
figures moving near it.

Ralph sketched a twining line from the bald
spot on which they stood down a slope, a
gully, through flowers, round and down to
the rock where the scar started.

"That's the quickest way back."

Eyes shining, mouths open, triumphant, they
savored the right of domination. They were
lifted up: were friends.

"There's no village smoke, and no boats,"
said Ralph wisely. "We'll make sure later;
but I think it's uninhabitated."

"We'll get food," cried Jack. "Hunt. Catch
things . . . until they fetch us."

Simon looked at them both, saying nothing
but nodding till his black hair flopped
backwards and forwards: his face was
glowing.

Ralph looked down the other way where there
was no reef.

"Steeper," said Jack.

Ralph made a cupping gesture.

"That bit of forest down there . . . the
mountain holds it up."

Every point of the mountain held up trees--
flowers and trees. Now the forest stirred,
roared, flailed. The nearer acres of rock
flowers fluttered and for half a minute the
breeze blew cool on their faces.

Ralph spread his arms.

"All ours."

They laughed and tumbled and shouted on
the mountain.

"I'm hungry."

When Simon mentioned his hunger the others
became aware of theirs.

"Come on," said Ralph. "We've found out
what we wanted to know."

They scrambled down a rock slope, dropped
among flowers and made their way under the
trees. Here they paused and examined the
bushes round them curiously.

Simon spoke first.

"Like candles. Candle bushes. Candle
buds."

The bushes were dark evergreen and aromatic
and the many buds were waxen green and
folded up against the light. Jack slashed
at one with his knife and the scent spilled
over them.

"Candle buds."

"You couldn't light them, " said Ralph.
"They just look like candles."

"Green candles," said Jack contemptuously.
"We can't eat them. Come on."

They were in the beginnings of the thick
forest, plonking with weary feet on a
track, when they heard the noises--squeak-
ings--and the hard strike of hoofs on a
path. As they pushed forward the squeaking
increased till it became a frenzy. They
found a piglet caught in a curtain of
creepers, throwing itself at the elastic
traces in all the madness of extreme terror.
Its voice was thin, needle-sharp and in-
sistent. The three boys rushed forward and
Jack drew his knife again with a flourish.
He raised his arm in the air. There came
a pause, a hiatus, the pig continued to
scream and the creepers to jerk, and the
blade continued to flash at the end of a
bony arm. The pause was only long enough
for them to understand what an enormity the
downward stroke would be. Then the piglet
tore loose from the creepers and scurried

into the undergrowth. They were left
looking at each other and the place of
terror. Jack's face was white under the
freckles. He noticed that he still held
the knife aloft and brought his arm down
replacing the blade in the sheath. Then
they all three laughed ashamedly and began
to climb back to the track.

"I was choosing a place," said Jack. "I
was just waiting for a moment to decide
where to stab him."

"You should stick a pig," said Ralph
fiercely. "They always talk about sticking
a pig."

"You cut a pig's throat to let the blood
out," said Jack, "otherwise you can't eat
the meat."

"Why didn't you--?"

They knew very well why he hadn't: because
of the enormity of the knife descending and
cutting into living flesh; because of the
unbearable blood.

"I was going to," said Jack. He was ahead
of them and they could not see his face.
"I was choosing a place. Next time--!"

He snatched his knife out of the sheath and
slammed it into a tree trunk. Next time
there would be no mercy. He looked round
fiercely, daring them to contradict. Then
they broke out into the sunlight and for a
while they were busy finding and devouring
food as they moved down the scar toward the
platform and the meeting.

CHAPTER TWO

FIRE ON THE MOUNTAIN

By the time Ralph finished blowing the conch
the platform was crowded. There were dif-
ferences between this meeting and the one
held in the morning. The afternoon sun
slanted in from the other side of the platform and most of the children, feeling too
late the smart of sunburn, had put their
clothes on. The choir, noticeably less of
a group, had discarded their cloaks.

Ralph sat on a fallen trunk, his left side
to the sun. On his right were most of the
choir; on his left the larger boys who had
not known each other before the evacuation;
before him small children squatted in the
grass.

Silence now. Ralph lifted the cream and
pink shell to his knees and a sudden breeze
scattered light over the platform. He was
uncertain whether to stand up or remain
sitting. He looked sideways to his left,
toward the bathing pool. Piggy was sitting
near but giving no help.

Ralph cleared his throat.

"Well then."

All at once he found he could talk fluently
and explain what he had to say. He passed
a hand through his fair hair and spoke.

"We're on an island. We've been on the
mountain top and seen water all round. We
saw no houses, no smoke, no footprints,
no boats, no people. We're on an uninhabitated island with no other people on
it."

Jack broke in.

"All the same you need an army--for hunting. Hunting pigs--"

"Yes. There are pigs on the island."

All three of them tried to convey the sense
of the pink live thing struggling in the
creepers.

"We saw--"

"Squealing--"

"It broke away--"

"Before I could kill it--but--next time!"

Jack slammed his knife into a trunk and
looked round challengingly.

The meeting settled down again.

"So you see," said Ralph, "we need hunters
to get us meat. And another thing."

He lifted the shell on his knees and looked
round the sun-slashed faces.

"There aren't any grownups. We shall have
to look after ourselves."

The meeting hummed and was silent.

"And another thing. We can't have everybody
talking at once. We'll have to have 'Hands
up' like at school."

He held the conch before his face and
glanced round the mouth.

"Then I'll give him the conch."

"Conch?"

"That's what this shell's called. I'll
give the conch to the next person to speak.
He can hold it when he's speaking."

"But--"

"Look--"

"And he won't be interrupted. Except by
me."

Jack was on his feet.

"We'll have rules!" he cried excitedly.
"Lots of rules! Then when anyone breaks
'em--"

"Whee-oh!"

"Wacco!"

"Bong!"

"Doink!"

Ralph felt the conch lifted from his lap.
Then Piggy was standing cradling the great

cream shell and the shouting died down.
Jack, left on his feet, looked uncertainly
at Ralph who smiled and patted the log.
Jack sat down. Piggy took off his glasses
and blinked at the assembly while he wiped
them on his shirt.

"You're hindering Ralph. You're not letting
him get to the most important thing."

He paused effectively.

"Who knows we're here? Eh?"

"They knew at the airport."

"The man with a trumpet-thing--"

"My dad."

Piggy put on his glasses.

"Nobody knows where we are," said Piggy.
He was paler than before and breathless.
"Perhaps they knew where we was going to;
and perhaps not. But they don't know
where we are 'cos we never got there."
He gaped at them for a moment, then swayed

and sat down.   Ralph took the conch from
his hands.

"That's what I was going to say," he went
on, "when you all, all. . . ." He gazed at
their intent faces. "The plane was shot
down in flames. Nobody knows where we are.
We may be here a long time."

The silence was so complete that they could
hear the unevenness of Piggy's breathing.
The sun slanted in and lay golden over
half the platform. The breezes that on the
lagoon had chased their tails like kittens
were finding their way across the platform
and into the forest. Ralph pushed back
the tangle of fair hair than hung on his
forehead.

"So we may be here a long time."

Nobody said anything. He grinned suddenly.

"But this is a good island. We--Jack,
Simon and me--we climbed the mountain.
It's wizard. There's food and drink,
and--"

"Rocks--"

"Blue flowers--"

Piggy, partly recovered, pointed to the conch in Ralph's hands, and Jack and Simon fell silent. Ralph went on.

"While we're waiting we can have a good time on this island."

He gesticulated widely.

"It's like in a book."

At once there was a clamor.

"Treasure Island--"

"Swallows and Amazons--"

"Coral Island--"

Ralph waved the conch.

"This is our island. It's a good island. Until the grownups come to fetch us we'll have fun."

Jack held out his hand for the conch.

"There's pigs," he said. "There's food;
and bathing water in that little stream
along there--and everything. Didn't anyone find anything else?"

He handed the conch back to Ralph and sat
down. Apparently no one had found anything.

The older boys first noticed the child when
he resisted. There was a group of little
boys urging him forward and he did not want
to go. He was a shrimp of a boy, about six
years old, and one side of his face was
blotted out by a mulberry-colored birthmark. He stood now, warped out of the per-
pendicular by the fierce light of publicity,
and he bored into the coarse grass with
one toe. He was muttering and about to cry.

The other little boys, whispering but serious, pushed him toward Ralph.

"All right," said Ralph, "come on then."

The small boy looked round in panic.

"Speak up!"

The small boy held out his hands for the conch and the assembly shouted with laughter; at once he snatched back his hands and started to cry.

"Let him have the conch!" shouted Piggy. "Let him have it!"

At last Ralph induced him to hold the shell but by then the blow of laughter had taken away the child's voice. Piggy knelt by him, one hand on the great shell, listening and interpreting to the assembly.

"He wants to know what you're going to do about the snake-thing."

Ralph laughed, and the other boys laughed with him. The small boy twisted further into himself.

"Tell us about the snake-thing."

"Now he says it was a beastie."

"Beastie?"

"A snake-thing. Ever so big. He saw it."

"Where?"

"In the woods."

Either the wandering breezes or perhaps
the decline of the sun allowed a little
coolness to lie under the trees. The boys
felt it and stirred restlessly.

"You couldn't have a beastie, a snake-
thing, on an island this size," Ralph explained kindly. "You only get them in big
countries, like Africa, or India."

Murmur; and the grave nodding of heads.

"He says the beastie came in the dark."

"Then he couldn't see it!"

Laughter and cheers.

"Did you hear that? Says he saw the thing
in the dark--"

"He still says he saw the beastie. It came
and went away again an' came back and wanted
to eat him--"

"He was dreaming."

Laughing, Ralph looked for confirmation
round the ring of faces. The older boys
agreed; but here and there among the little
ones was the doubt that required more than
rational assurance.

"He must have had a nightmare. Stumbling
about among all those creepers."

More grave nodding; they knew about nightmares.

"He says he saw the beastie, the snake-
thing, and will it come back tonight?"

"But there isn't a beastie!"

"He says in the morning it turned into
them things like ropes in the trees and
hung in the branches. He says will it come
back tonight?"

"But there isn't a beastie!"

There was no laughter at all now and more
grave watching. Ralph pushed both hands

through his hair and looked at the little
boy in mixed amusement and exasperation.

Jack seized the conch.

"Ralph's right of course. There isn't a
snake-thing. But if there was a snake
we'd hunt it and kill it. We're going to
hunt pigs to get meat for everybody. And
we'll look for the snake too--"

"But there isn't a snake!"

"We'll make sure when we go hunting."

Ralph was annoyed and, for the moment,
defeated. He felt himself facing something
ungraspable. The eyes that looked so intently at him were without humor.

"But there isn't a beast!"

Something he had not known was there rose
in him and compelled him to make the point,
loudly and again.

"But I tell you there isn't a beast!"

The assembly was silent.

Ralph lifted the conch again and his good
humor came back as he thought of what he
had to say next.

"Now we come to the most important thing.
I've been thinking. I was thinking while
we were climbing the mountain." He flashed
a conspiratorial grin at the other two.
"And on the beach just now. This is what I
thought. We want to have fun. And we want
to be rescued."

The passionate noise of agreement from the
assembly hit him like a wave and he lost
his thread. He thought again.

"We want to be rescued; and of course we
shall be rescued."

Voices babbled. The simple statement, un-
backed by any proof but the weight of
Ralph's new authority, brought light and
happiness. He had to wave the conch before
he could make them hear him.

"My father's in the Navy. He said there
aren't any unknown islands left. He says
the Queen has a big room full of maps and

all the islands in the world are drawn
there. So the Queen's got a picture of
this island."

Again came the sounds of cheerfulness and
better heart.

"And sooner or later a ship will put in
here. It might even be Daddy's ship. So
you see, sooner or later, we shall be
rescued."

He paused, with the point made. The assembly was lifted toward safety by his words.
They liked and now respected him. Spon-
taneously they began to clap and presently
the platform was loud with applause. Ralph
flushed, looking sideways at Piggy's open
admiration, and then the other way at Jack
who was smirking and showing that he too
knew how to clap.

Ralph waved the conch.

"Shut up! Wait! Listen!"

He went on in the silence, born on his
triumph.

"There's another thing. We can help them
to find us. If a ship comes near the island
they may not notice us. So we must make
smoke on top of the mountain. We must make
a fire."

"A fire! Make a fire!"

At once half the boys were on their feet.
Jack clamored among them, the conch forgotten.

"Come on! Follow me!"

The space under the palm trees was full of
noise and movement. Ralph was on his feet
too, shouting for quiet, but no one heard
him. All at once the crowd swayed toward
the island and was gone--following Jack.
Even the tiny children went and did their
best among the leaves and broken branches.
Ralph was left, holding the conch, with
no one but Piggy.

Piggy's breathing was quite restored.

"Like kids!" he said scornfully. "Acting
like a crowd of kids!"

Ralph looked at him doubtfully and laid the conch on the tree trunk.

"I bet it's gone tea-time," said Piggy. "What do they think they're going to do on that mountain?"

He caressed the shell respectfully, then stopped and looked up.

"Ralph! Hey! Where you going?"

Ralph was already clambering over the first smashed swathes of the scar. A long way ahead of him was crashing and laughter.

Piggy watched him in disgust.

"Like a crowd of kids--"

He sighed, bent, and laced up his shoes. The noise of the errant assembly faded up the mountain. Then, with the martyred expression of a parent who has to keep up with the senseless ebullience of the children, he picked up the conch, turned toward the forest, and began to pick his way over the tumbled scar.

Below the other side of the mountain top
was a platform of forest. Once more Ralph
found himself making the cupping gesture.

"Down there we could get as much wood as
we want."

Jack nodded and pulled at his underlip.
Starting perhaps a hundred feet below them
on the steeper side of the mountain, the
patch might have been designed expressly
for fuel. Trees, forced by the damp heat,
found too little soil for full growth, fell
early and decayed: creepers cradled them,
and new saplings searched a way up.

Jack turned to the choir, who stood ready.
Their black caps of maintenance were slid
over one ear like berets.

"We'll build a pile. Come on."

They found the likliest path down and began
tugging at the dead wood. And the small
boys who had reached the top came sliding
too till everyone but Piggy was busy. Most
of the wood was so rotten that when they
pulled it broke up into a shower of frag-
ments and woodlice and decay; but some

trunks came out in one piece. The twins,
Sam 'n Eric, were the first to get a likely
log but they could do nothing till Ralph,
Jack, Simon, Roger and Maurice found room
for a hand-hold. Then they inched the
grotesque dead thing up the rock and toppled
it over on top. Each party of boys added a
quota, less or more, and the pile grew. At
the return Ralph found himself alone on a
limb with Jack and they grinned at each
other, sharing this burden. Once more,
amid the breeze, the shouting, the slanting
sunlight on the high mountain, was shed
that glamour, that strange invisible light
of friendship, adventure, and contest.

"Almost too heavy."

Jack grinned back.

"Not for the two of us."

Together, joined in effort by the burden,
they staggered up the last steep of the
mountain. Together, they chanted One!
Two! Three! and crashed the log on to the
great pile. Then they stepped back, laughing with triumphant pleasure, so that immediately Ralph had to stand on his head.

Below them, boys were still laboring, though
some of the small ones had lost interest
and were searching this new forest for
fruit. Now the twins, with unsuspected
intelligence, came up the mountain with
armfuls of dried leaves and dumped them
against the pile. One by one, as they
sensed that the pile was complete, the boys
stopped going back for more and stood, with
the pink, shattered top of the mountain
round them. Breath came evenly by now, and
sweat dried.

Ralph and Jack looked at each other while
society paused about them. The shameful
knowledge grew in them and they did not
know how to begin confession.

Ralph spoke first, crimson in the face.

"Will you?"

He cleared his throat and went on.

"Will you light the fire?"

Now the absurd situation was open, Jack
blushed too. He began to mutter vaguely.

"You rub two sticks. You rub--"

He glanced at Ralph, who blurted out the last confession of incompetence.

"Has anyone got any matches?"

"You make a bow and spin the arrow," said Roger. He rubbed his hands in mime. "Psss. Psss."

A little air was moving over the mountain. Piggy came with it, in shorts and shirt, laboring cautiously out of the forest with the evening sunlight gleaming from his glasses. He held the conch under his arm.

Ralph shouted at him.

"Piggy! Have you got any matches?"

The other boys took up the cry till the mountain rang. Piggy shook his head and came to the pile.

"My! You've make a big heap, haven't you?"

Jack pointed suddenly.

"His specs--use them as burning glasses!"

Piggy was surrounded before he could back away.

"Here--let me go!" His voice rose to a shriek of terror as Jack snatched the glasses off his face. "Mind out! Give 'em back! I can hardly see! You'll break the conch!"

Ralph elbowed him to one side and knelt by the pile.

"Stand out of the light."

There was pushing and pulling and officious cries. Ralph moved the lenses back and forth, this way and that, till a glossy white image of the declining sun lay on a piece of rotten wood. Almost at once a thin trickle of smoke rose up and made him cough. Jack knelt too and blew gently, so that the smoke drifted away, thickening, and a tiny flame appeared. The flame, nearly invisible at first in that bright sunlight, enveloped a small twig, grew, was enriched with color and reached up to a

branch which exploded with a sharp crack.
The flame flapped higher and the boys broke
into a cheer.

"My specs!" howled Piggy. "Give me my
specs!"

Ralph stood away from the pile and put the
glasses into Piggy's grouping hands. His
voice subsided to a mutter.

"Jus' blurs, that's all. Hardly see my
hand--"

The boys were dancing. The pile was so
rotten, and now so tinder-dry, that whole
limbs yielded passionately to the yellow
flames that poured upwards and shook a
great beard of flame twenty feet in the
air. For yards round the fire the heat was
like a blow, and the breeze was a river of
sparks. Trunks crumbled to white dust.

Ralph shouted.

"More wood! All of you get more wood!"

Life became a race with the fire and the

boys scattered through the upper forest.
To keep a clean flay of flame flying on
the mountain was the immediate end and no
one looked further. Even the smallest boys,
unless fruit claimed them, brought little
pieces of wood and threw them in. The air
moved a little faster and became a light
wind, so that leeward and windward side
were clearly differentiated. On one side
the air was cool, but on the other the fire
thrust out a savage arm of heat that
crinkled hair on the instant. Boys who
felt the evening wind on their damp faces
paused to enjoy the freshness of it and
then found they were exhausted. They flung
themselves down in the shadows that lay
among the shattered rocks. The beard of
flame diminished quickly; then the pile
fell inwards with a soft, cindery sound, and
sent a great tree of sparks upwards that
leaned away and drifted downwind. The boys
lay, panting like dogs.

Ralph raised his head off his forearms.

"That was no good."

Roger spat efficiently into the hot dust.

"What d'you mean?"

"There wasn't any smoke. Only flame."

Piggy had settled himself in a space between two rocks, and sat with the conch on
his knees.

"We haven't made a fire," he said, "what's
any use. We couldn't keep a fire like that
going, not if we tried."

"A fat lot you tried," said Jack contemptuously. "You just sat."

"We used his specs," said Simon, smearing
a black cheek with his forearm. "He helped
that way."

"I got the conch," said Piggy indignantly.
"You let me speak!"

"The conch doesn't count on top of the
mountain," said Jack, "so you shut up."

"I got the conch in my hand."

"Put on green branches," said Maurice.
"That's the best way to make smoke."

"I got the conch--"

Jack turned fiercely.

"You shut up!"

Piggy wilted. Ralph took the conch from
him and looked round the circle of boys.

"We've got to have special people for
looking after the fire. Any day there may
be a ship out there"--he waved his arm at
the taut wire of the horizon--"and if we
have a signal going they'll come and take
us off. And another thing. We ought to
have more rules. Where the conch is,
that's a meeting. The same up here as down
there."

They assented. Piggy opened his mouth to
speak, caught Jack's eye and shut it again.
Jack held out his hands for the conch and
stood up, holding the delicate thing carefully in his sooty hands.

"I agree with Ralph. We've got to have
rules and obey them. After all, we're not
savages. We're English, and the English

are best at everything. So we've got to
do the right things."

He turned to Ralph.

"Ralph, I'll split up the choir--my hunters,
that is--into groups, and we'll be responsible for keeping the fire going--"

This generosity brought a spatter of applause from the boys, so that Jack grinned
at them, then waved the conch for silence.

"We'll let the fire burn out now. Who
would see smoke at night-time, anyway? And
we can start the fire again whenever we
like.   Altos--you can keep the fire going
this week, and trebles the next--"

The assembly assented gravely.

"And we'll be responsible for keeping a
lookout too. If we see a ship out there"--
they followed the direction of his bony arm
with their eyes--"we'll put green branches
on. Then there'll be more smoke."

They gazed intently at the dense blue of

the horizon, as if a little silhouette might
appear there at any moment.

The sun in the west was a drop of burning
gold that slid nearer and nearer the sill
of the world. All at once they were aware
of the evening as the end of light and
warmth.

Roger took the conch and looked round at
them gloomily.

"I've been watching the sea. There hasn't
been the trace of a ship. Perhaps we'll
never be rescued."

A murmur rose and swept away. Ralph took
back the conch.

"I said before we'll be rescued sometime.
"We've just got to wait, that's all."

Daring, indignant, Piggy took the conch.

"That's what I said! I said about our
meetings and things and then you said
shut up--"

His voice lifted into the whine of virtuous
recrimination. They stirred and began to
shout him down.

"You said you wanted a small fire and you
been and built a pile like a hayrick. If
I say anything," cried Piggy, with bitter
realism, "you say shut up; but if Jack or
Maurice or Simon--"

He paused in the tumult, standing, looking
beyond them and down the unfriendly side of
the mountain to the great patch where they
had found dead wood. Then he laughed so
strangely that they were hushed, looking
at the flash of his spectacles in astonishment. They followed his gaze to find the
sour joke.

"You got your small fire all right."

Smoke was rising here and there among the
creepers that festooned the dead or dying
trees. As they watched, a flash of fire
appeared at the root of one wisp, and then
the smoke thickened. Small flames stirred
at the trunk of a tree and crawled away
through leaves and brushwood, diving and

increasing. One patch touched a tree trunk
and scrambled up like a bright squirrel.
The smoke increased, sifted, rolled out-
wards. The squirrel leapt on the wings of
the wind and clung to another standing
tree, eating downwards. Beneath the dark
canopy of leaves and smoke the fire laid
hold on the forest and began to gnaw. Acres
of black and yellow smoke rolled steadily
toward the sea. At the sight of the flames
and the irresistible course of the fire,
the boys broke into shrill, excited cheer-
ing. The flames, as though they were a
kind of wild life, crept as a jaguar creeps
on its belly toward a line of birch-like
saplings that fledged an outcrop of the pink
rock. They flapped at the first of the
trees, and the branches grew a brief foliage
of fire. The heart of flame leapt nimbly
across the gap between the trees and then
went swinging and flaring along the whole
row of them. Beneath the capering boys a
quarter of a mile square of forest was
savage with smoke and flame. The separate
noises of the fire merged into a drum-roll
that seemed to shake the mountain.

"You got your small fire all right."

Startled, Ralph realized that the boys were
falling still and silent, feeling the beginnings of awe at the power set free below
them. The knowledge and the awe made him
savage.

"Oh, shut up!"

"I got the conch," said Piggy, in a hurt
voice. "I got a right to speak."

They looked at him with eyes that lacked
interest in what they saw, and cocked ears
at the drum-roll of the fire. Piggy glanced
nervously into hell and cradled the conch.

"We got to let that burn out now. And that
was our firewood."
He licked his lips.

"There ain't nothing we can do. We ought
to be more careful. I'm scared--"

Jack dragged his eyes away from the fire.

"You're always scared. Yah--Fatty!"
"I got the conch," said Piggy bleakly. He

turned to Ralph. "I got the conch, ain't
I Ralph?"

Unwillingly Ralph turned away from the
splendid, awful sight.

"What's that?"

"The conch. I got a right to speak."

The twins giggled together.

"We wanted smoke--"

"Now look--!"

A pall stretched for miles away from the
island. All the boys except Piggy started
to giggle; presently they were shrieking
with laughter.

Piggy lost his temper.

"I got the conch! Just you listen! The
first thing we ought to have made was
shelters down there by the beach. It
wasn't half cold down there in the night.
But the first time Ralph says 'fire' you

goes howling and screaming up this here
mountain. Like a pack of kids!"

By now they were listening to the tirade.

"How can you expect to be rescued if you
don't put first things first and act
proper?"

He took off his glasses and made as if to
put down the conch; but the sudden motion
toward it of most of the older boys changed
his mind. He tucked the shell under his
arm, and crouched back on a rock.

"Then when you get here you build a bonfire
that isn't no use. Now you been and set
the whole island on fire. Won't we look
funny if the whole island burns up? Cooked
fruit, that's what we'll have to eat, and
roast pork. And that's nothing to laugh
at! You said Ralph was chief and you don't
give him time to think. Then when he says
something you rush off, like, like--"

He paused for breath, and the fire growled
at them.

"And that's not all. Them kids. The little
'uns. Who took any notice of 'em? Who
knows how many we got?"

Ralph took a sudden step forward.

"I told you to. I told you to get a list
of names!"

"How could I," cried Piggy indignantly,
"all by myself? They waited for two minutes, then they fell in the sea; they went
into the forest; they just scattered everywhere. How was I to know which was which?"

Ralph licked pale lips.

"Then you don't know how many of us there
ought to be?"

"How could I with them little 'uns running
round like insects? Then when you three
came back, as soon as you said make a fire,
they all ran away, and I never had a chance
--"

"That's enough!" said Ralph sharply, and
snatched back the conch. "If you didn't
you didn't."

"--then you come up here an' pinch my
specs--"

Jack turned on him.

"You shut up!"

"--and them little 'uns was wandering about
down there where the fire is. How d'you
know they aren't still there?"

Piggy stood up and pointed to the smoke and
flames. A murmur rose among the boys and
died away. Something strange was happening
to Piggy, for he was gasping for breath.

"That little 'un--" gasped Piggy--" him
with the mark on his face, I don't see him.
Where is he now?"

The crowd was as silent as death.

"Him that talked about the snakes. He was
down there--"

A tree exploded in the fire like a bomb.
Tall swathes of creepers rose for a moment
into view, agonized, and went down again.
The little boys screamed at them.

"Snakes! Snakes! Look at the snakes!"

In the west, and unheeded, the sun lay only
an inch or two above the sea. Their faces
were lit redly from beneath. Piggy fell
against a rock and clutched it with both
hands.

"That little 'un that had a mark on his
face--where is--he now? I tell you I don't
see him."

The boys looked at each other fearfully,
unbelieving. "--where is he now?"

Ralph muttered the reply as if in shame.

"Perhaps he went back to the, the--"

Beneath them, on the unfriendly side of
the mountain, the drum-roll continued.

CHAPTER THREE

HUTS ON THE BEACH

Jack was bent double. He was down like
a sprinter, his nose only a few inches from
the humid earth. The tree trunks and the
creepers that festooned them lost themselves
in a green dusk thirty feet above him, and
all about was the undergrowth. There was
only the faintest indication of a trail
here; a cracked twig and what might be the
impression of one side of a hoof. He lowered his chin and stared at the traces as
though he would force them to speak to him.
Then dog-like, uncomfortably on all fours
yet unheeding his discomfort, he stole
forward five yards and stopped. Here was
loop of creeper with a tendril pendant from
a node. The tendril was polished on the
underside; pigs, passing through the loop,
brushed it with their bristly hide.

Jack crouched with his face a few inches
away from this clue, then stared forward
into the semi-darkness of the undergrowth.
His sandy hair considerably longer than it
had been when they dropped in, was lighter

now; and his bare back was a mass of dark
freckles and peeling sunburn. A sharpened
stick about five feet long trailed from
his right hand, and except for a pair of
tattered shorts held up by his knife-belt
he was naked. He closed his eyes, raised
his head and breathed in gently with flared
nostrils, assessing the current of warm air
for information. The forest and he were
very still.

At length he let out his breath in a long
sigh and opened his eyes. They were bright
blue, eyes that in this frustration seemed
bolting and nearly mad. He passed his
tongue across dry lips and scanned the un-
communicative forest. Then again he stole
forward and cast this way and that over the
ground.

The silence of the forest was more oppressive than the heat, and at this hour of the
day there was not even the whine of insects.
Only when Jack himself roused a gaudy bird
from a primitive nest of sticks was the
silence shattered and echoes set ringing by
a harsh cry that seemed to come out of the
abyss of ages. Jack himself shrank at this

cry with a hiss of indrawn breath, and for
a minute became less a hunter than a furtive
thing, ape-like among the tangle of trees.
Then the trail, the frustration, claimed him
again and he searched the ground avidly.
By the trunk of a vast tree that grew pale
flowers on its grey bark he checked, closed
his eyes, and once more drew in the warm
air; and this time his breath came short,
there was even a passing pallor in his face,
and then the surge of blood again. He
passed like a shadow under the darkness of
the tree and crouched, looking down at the
trodden ground at his feet.

The droppings were warm. They lay piled
among turned earth. They were olive green,
smooth, and they steamed a little. Jack
lifted his head and stared at the inscru-
table masses of creeper that lay across
the trail. Then he raised his spear and
sneaked forward. Beyond the creeper, the
trail joined a pig-run that was wide enough
and trodden enough to be a path. The ground
was hardened by an accustomed tread and as
Jack rose to his full height he heard something moving on it. He swung back his
right arm and hurled the spear with all his

strength. From the pig-run came the quick,
hard patter of hoofs, a castanet sound,
seductive, maddening--the promise of meat.
He rushed out of the undergrowth and
snatched up his spear. The pattering of
pig's trotters died away in the distance.

Jack stood there, streaming with sweat,
streaked with brown earth, stained by all
the vicissitudes of a day's hunting. Swear-
ing, he turned off the trail and pushed his
way through until the forest opened a little
and instead of bald trunks supporting a
dark roof there were light grey trunks and
crowns of feathery palm. Beyond these was
the glitter of the sea and he could hear
voices. Ralph was standing by a contraption
of palm trunks and leaves, a rude shelter
that faced the lagoon and seemed very near
to falling down. He did not notice when
Jack spoke.

"Got any water?"

Ralph looked up, frowning, from the com-
plication of leaves. He did not notice
Jack even when he saw him.

"I said have you got any water? I'm
thirsty."

Ralph withdrew his attention from the shelter and realized Jack with a start.

"Oh, hullo. Water? There by the tree.
Ought to be some left."

Jack took up a coconut shell that brimmed
with fresh water from among a group that
was arranged in the shade, and drank. The
water splashed over his chin and neck and
chest. He breathed noisily when he had
finished.

"Needed that."

Simon spoke from inside the shelter.

"Up a bit."

Ralph turned to the shelter and lifted a
branch with a whole tiling of leaves.

The leaves came apart and fluttered down.
Simon's contrite face appeared in the hole.

"Sorry."

Ralph surveyed the wreck with distaste.

"Never get it done."

He flung himself down at Jack's feet.
Simon remained, looking out of the hole in
the shelter. Once down, Ralph explained.

"Been working for days now. And look!"

Two shelters were in position, but shaky.
This one was a ruin.

"And they keep running off. You remember
the meeting? How everyone was going to
work hard until the shelters were finished?"

"Except me and my hunters--"

"Except the hunters. Well, the littluns
are--"

He gesticulated, sought for a word.

"They're hopeless. The older ones aren't
much better. D'you see? All day I've been
working with Simon. No one else. They're
off bathing, or eating, or playing."

Simon poked his head out carefully.

"You're chief. You tell 'em off."

Ralph lay flat and looked up at the palm
trees and the sky.

"Meetings. Don't we love meetings? Every
day. Twice a day. We talk." He got on
one elbow. "I bet if I blew the conch this
minute, they'd come running. Then we'd be
you know, very solemn, and someone would
say we ought to build a jet, or a submarine,
or a TV set. When the meeting was over
they'd work for five minutes, then wander
off or go hunting."

Jack flushed.

"We want meat."

"Well, we haven't got any yet. And we want
shelters. Besides, the rest of your hunters
came back hours ago. They've been swimming."

"I went on," said Jack. "I let them go.
I had to go on. I--"

He tried to convey the compulsion to track
down and kill that was swallowing him up.

"I went on. I thought, by myself--"

The madness came into his eyes again.

"I thought I might kill."

"But you didn't."

"I thought I might."

Some hidden passion vibrated in Ralph's
voice.

"But you haven't yet."

His invitation might have passed as casual,
were it not for the undertone.

"You wouldn't care to help with the shelters, I suppose?"

"We want meat--"

"And we don't get it."

Now the antagonism was audible.

"But I shall! Next time! I've got to get
a barb on this spear! We wounded a pig and
the spear fell out. If we could only make
barbs--"

"We need shelters."

Suddenly Jack shouted in rage.

"Are you accusing--?"

"All I'm saying is we've worked dashed
hard. That's all."

They were both red in the face and found
looking at each other difficult. Ralph
rolled on his stomach and began to play
with the grass.

"If it rains like when we dropped in we'll
need shelters all right. And then another
thing. We need shelters because of the--"

He paused for a moment and they both pushed
their anger away. Then he went on with the
safe, changed subject.

"You've noticed, haven't you?"

Jack put down his spear and squatted.

"Noticed what?"

"Well. They're frightened."

He rolled over and peered into Jack's
fierce, dirty face.

"I mean the way things are. They dream.
You can hear 'em. Have you been awake at
night?"

Jack shook his head.

"They talk and scream. The littluns. Even
some of the others. As if--"

"As if it wasn't a good island."

Astonished at the interruption, they looked
up at Simon's serious face.

"As if," said Simon, "the beastie, the
beastie or the snake-thing, was real.
Remember?"

The two older boys flinched when they heard

the shameful syllable. Snakes were not
mentioned now, were not mentionable.

"As if this wasn't a good island," said
Ralph slowly. "Yes, that's right."

Jack sat up and stretched out his legs.

"They're batty."

"Crackers. Remember when we went exploring?"

They grinned at each other, remembering the
glamour of the first day. Ralph went on.

"So we need shelters as a sort of--"

"Home."

"That's right."

Jack drew up his legs, clasped his knees,
and frowned in an effort to attain clarity.

"All the same--in the forest. I mean when
you're hunting, not when you're getting
fruit, of course, but when you're on your
own--"

He paused for a moment, not sure if Ralph
would take him seriously.

"Go on."

"If you're hunting sometimes you catch yourself feeling as if--" He flushed suddenly.
"There's nothing in it of course. Just a
feeling. But you can feel as if you're not
hunting, but--being hunted, as if something's behind you all the time in the
jungle."

They were silent again: Simon intent, Ralph
incredulous and faintly indignant. He sat
up, rubbing one shoulder with a dirty hand.

"Well, I don't know."

Jack leapt to his feet and spoke very
quickly.

"That's how you can feel in the forest. Of
course there's nothing in it. Only--only
--"

He took a few rapid steps toward the beach,
then came back.

"Only I know how they feel. See? That's
all."

"The best thing we can do is get ourselves
rescued."

Jack had to think for a moment before he
could remember what rescue was.

"Rescue? Yes, of course! All the same,
I'd like to catch a pig first--" He
snatched up his spear and dashed it into
the ground. The opaque, mad look came into
his eyes again. Ralph looked at him crit-
ically through his tangle of fair hair.

"So long as your hunters remember the fire
--"

"You and your fire!"

The two boys trotted down the beach, and,
turning at the water's edge, looked back
at the pink mountain. The trickle of smoke
sketched a chalky line up the solid blue of
the sky, wavered high up and faded. Ralph
frowned.

"I wonder how far off you could see that."

"Miles"

"We don't make enough smoke."

The bottom part of the trickle, as though
conscious of their gaze, thickened to a
creamy blur which crept up the feeble
column.

"They've put on green branches," muttered
Ralph. "I wonder!" He screwed up his
eyes and swung round to search the horizon.

"Got it!"

Jack shouted so loudly that Ralph jumped.

"What? Where? Is it a ship?"

But Jack was pointing to the high decliv-
ities that led down from the mountain to
the flatter part of the island.

"Of course! They'll lie up there--they
must, when the sun's too hot--"

Ralph gazed bewildered at his rapt face.

"--they get up high. High up and in the
shade, resting during the heat, like cows
at home--"

"I thought you saw a ship!"

"We could steal up on one--paint our faces
so they wouldn't see--perhaps surround them
and then--"

Indignation took away Ralph's control.

"I was talking about smoke! Don't you want
to be rescued? All you can talk about is
pig, pig, pig!"

"But we want meat!"

"And I work all day with nothing but Simon
and you come back and don't even notice
the huts!"

"I was working too--"

"But you like it!" shouted Ralph. "You
want to hunt! While I--"

They faced each other on the bright beach,

astonished at the rub of feeling. Ralph
looked away first, pretending interest in
a group of littluns on the sand. From
beyond the platform came the shouting of
the hunters in the swimming pool. On the
end of the platform Piggy was lying flat,
looking down into the brilliant water.

"People don't help much."

He wanted to explain how people were never
quite what they thought they were.

"Simon. He helps." He pointed at the
shelters.

"All the rest rushed off. He's done as
much as I have. Only--"

"Simon's always about."

Ralph started back to the shelters with
Jack by his side.

"Do a bit for you," muttered Jack, "before
I have a bathe."

"Don't bother."

But when they reached the shelters Simon
was not to be seen. Ralph put his head in
the hole, withdrew it, and turned to Jack.

"He's buzzed off."

"Got fed up," said Jack, "and gone for a
bathe."

Ralph frowned.

"He's queer. He's funny."

Jack nodded, as much for the sake of
agreeing as anything, and by tacit consent
they left the shelter and went toward the
bathing pool.

"And then," said Jack, "when I've had a
bathe and something to eat, I'll just trek
over to the other side of the mountain and
see if I can see any traces. Coming?"

"But the sun's nearly set!"

"I might have time--"

They walked along, two continents of ex-
perience and feeling, unable to communicate.

"If I could only get a pig!"

"I'll come back and go on with the shelter."

They looked at each other, baffled, in love and hate. All the warm salt water of the bathing pool and the shouting and splashing and laughing were only just sufficient to bring them together again.

Simon was not in the bathing pool as they had expected.

When the other two had trotted down the beach to look back at the mountain he had followed them for a few yards and then stopped. He had stood frowning down at a pile of sand on the beach where somebody had been trying to build a little house or hut. Then he turned his back on this and walked into the forest with an air of purpose. He was a small, skinny boy, his chin pointed, and his eyes so bright they had deceived Ralph into thinking him de-lightfully gay and wicked. The coarse mop of black hair was long and swung down, almost concealing a low, broad forehead.

He wore the remains of shorts and his feet
were bare like Jack's. Always darkish in
color, Simon was burned by the sun to a
deep tan that glistened with sweat.

He picked his way up the scar, passed the
great rock where Ralph had climbed on the
first morning, then turned off to his right
among the trees. He walked with an accustomed tread through the acres of fruit
trees, where the least energetic could find
an easy if unsatisfying meal. Flower and
fruit grew together on the same tree and
everywhere was the scent of ripeness and
the booming of a million bees at pasture.
Here the littluns who had run after him
caught up with him. They talked, cried
out unintelligibly, lugged him toward the
trees. Then, amid the roar of bees in the
afternoon sunlight, Simon found for them
the fruit they could not reach, pulled off
the choicest from up in the foliage, passed
them back down to the endless, outstretched
hands. When he had satisfied them he paused
and looked round. The littluns watched him
inscrutably over double handfuls of ripe
fruit.

Simon turned away from them and went where
the just perceptible path led him. Soon
high jungle closed in. Tall trunks bore
unexpected pale flowers all the way up to
the dark canopy where life went on clamor-
ously. The air here was dark too, and the
creepers dropped their ropes like the rig-
ging of foundered ships. His feet left
prints in the soft soil and the creepers
shivered throughout their lengths when he
bumped them.

He came at last to a place where more sun-
shine fell. Since they had not so far to
go for light the creepers had woven a great
mat that hung at the side of an open space
in the jungle; for here a patch of rock
came close to the surface and would not
allow more than little plants and ferns to
grow. The whole space was walled with dark
aromatic bushes, and was a bowl of heat and
light. A great tree, fallen across one
corner, leaned against the trees that still
stood and a rapid climber flaunted red and
yellow sprays right to the top.

Simon paused. He looked over his shoulder
as Jack had done at the close ways behind

him and glanced swiftly round to confirm
that he was utterly alone. For a moment
his movements were almost furtive. Then he
bent down and wormed his way into the center
of the mat. The creepers and the bushes
were so close that he left his sweat on them
and they pulled together behind him. When
he was secure in the middle he was in a
little cabin screened off from the open
space by a few leaves. He squatted down,
parted the leaves and looked out into the
clearing. Nothing moved but a pair of gaudy
butterflies that danced round each other in
the hot air. Holding his breath he cocked
a critical ear at the sounds of the island.
Evening was advancing toward the island;
the sounds of the bright fantastic birds,
the bee-sounds, even the crying of the gulls
that were returning to their roosts among
the square rocks, were fainter. The deep
sea breaking miles away on the reef made an
undertone less perceptible than the sussur-
ration of the blood.

Simon dropped the screen of leaves back
into place. The slope of the bars of honey-
colored sunlight decreased; they slid up
the bushes, passed over the green candle-
like buds, moved up toward the canopy, and

darkness thickened under the trees. With
the fading of the light the riotous colors
died and the heat and urgency cooled away.
The candle-buds stirred. Their green
sepals drew back a little and the white tips
of the flowers rose delicately to meet the
open air.

Now the sunlight had lifted clear of the
open space and withdrawn from the sky.
Darkness poured out, submerging the ways
between the trees till they were dim and
strange as the bottom of the sea. The
candle-buds opened their wide white flowers
glimmering under the light that pricked
down from the first stars. Their scent
spilled out into the air and took possession
of the island.

CHAPTER FOUR

PAINTED FACES AND LONG HAIR

The first rhythm that they became used to
was the slow swing from dawn to quick dusk.
They accepted the pleasures of morning, the
bright sun, the whelming sea and sweet air,
as a time when play was good and life so
full that hope was not necessary and therefore forgotten. Toward noon, as the floods
of light fell more nearly to the perpendic-
ular, the stark colors of the morning were
smoothed in pearl and opalescence; and the
heat--as though the impending sun's height
gave it momentum--became a blow that they
ducked, running to the shade and lying
there, perhaps even sleeping.

Strange things happened at midday. The
glittering sea rose up, moved apart in
planes of blatant impossibility; the coral
reef and the few stunted palms that clung
to the more elevated parts would float up
into the sky, would quiver, be plucked
apart, run like raindrops on a wire or be
repeated as in an odd succession of mirrors.
Sometimes land loomed where there was no

land and flicked out like a bubble as the
children watched. Piggy discounted all
this learnedly as a "mirage"; and since no
boy could reach even the reef over the
stretch of water where the snapping sharks
waited, they grew accustomed to these mys-
teries and ignored them, just as they ignored the miraculous, throbbing stars. At
midday the illusions merged into the sky and
there the sun gazed down like an angry eye.
Then, at the end of the afternoon, the
mirage subsided and the horizon became
level and blue and clipped as the sun de-
clined. That was another time of compara-
tive coolness but menaced by the coming of
the dark. When the sun sank darkness
dripped on the island like an extinguisher
and soon the shelters were full of rest-
lessness, under the remote stars.

Nevertheless, the northern European tradi-
tion of work, play, and food right through
the day, made it impossible for them to
adjust themselves wholly to this new rhythm.
The littlun Percival had early crawled into
a shelter and stayed there for two days,
talking, singing, and crying, till they
thought him batty and were faintly amused.

Ever since then he had been peaked, red-
eyed, and miserable; a littlun who played
little and cried often.

The smaller boys were known now by the
generic title of "littluns." The decrease
in size, from Ralph down, was gradual; and
though there was a dubious region inhabited
by Simon and Robert and Maurice, nevertheless no one had any difficulty in recogniz-
ing biguns at one end and littluns at the
other. The undoubted littluns, those aged
about six, led a quite distinct, and at the
same time intense, life of their own. They
ate most of the day, picking fruit where
they could reach it and not particular
about ripeness and quality. They were used
now to stomach-aches and a sort of chronic
diarrhoea. They suffered untold terrors
in the dark and huddled together for com-
fort. Apart from food and sleep, they found
time for play, aimless and trivial, in the
white sand by the bright water. They cried
for their mothers much less often than might
have been expected; they were very brown,
and filthily dirty. They obeyed the summons
of the conch, partly because Ralph blew it,
and he was big enough to be a link with the

adult world of authority; and partly because
they enjoyed the entertainment of the
assemblies. But otherwise they seldom
bothered with the biguns and their passionately emotional and corporate life was
their own.

They had built castles in the sand at the
bar of the little river. These castles
were about one foot high and were decorated
with shells, withered flowers, and inter-
esting stones. Round the castles was a
complex of marks, tracks, walls, railway
lines, that were of significance only if
inspected with the eye at beach-level. The
littluns played here, if not happily at
least with absorbed attention; and often
as many as three of them would play the
same game together.

Three were playing here now. Henry was the
biggest of them. He was also a distant
relative of that other boy whose mulberry-
marked face had not been seen since the
evening of the great fire; but he was not
old enough to understand this, and if he
had been told that the other boy had gone
home in an aircraft, he would have accepted
the statement without fuss or disbelief.

Henry was a bit of a leader this afternoon,
because the other two were Percival and
Johnny, the smallest boys on the island.
Percival was mouse-colored and had not been
very attractive even to his mother; Johnny
was well built, with fair hair and a natural
belligerence. Just now he was being obedient because he was interested; and the
three children, kneeling in the sand, were
at peace.

Roger and Maurice came out of the forest.
They were relieved from duty at the fire
and had come down for a swim. Roger led
the way straight through the castles, kicking them over, burying the flowers, scat-
tering the chosen stones. Maurice followed,
laughing, and added to the destruction.
The three littluns paused in their game and
looked up. As it happened, the particular
marks in which they were interested had not
been touched, so they made no protest. Only
Percival began to whimper with an eyeful of
sand and Maurice hurried away. In his other
life Maurice had received chastisement for
filling a younger eye with sand. Now,
though there was no parent to let fall a
heavy hand, Maurice still felt the unease

of wrong-doing. At the back of his mind
formed the uncertain outlines of an excuse.
He muttered something about a swim and
broke into a trot.

Roger remained, watching the littluns. He
was not noticeably darker than when he had
dropped in, but the shock of black hair,
down his nape and low on his forehead,
seemed to suit his gloomy face and made what
had seemed at first an unsociable remoteness
into something forbidding. Percival finished his whimper and went on playing, for
the tears had washed the sand away. Johnny
watched him with china-blue eyes; then
began to fling up sand in a shower, and
presently Percival was crying again.

When Henry tired of his play and wandered
off along the beach, Roger followed him,
keeping beneath the palms and drifting
casually in the same direction. Henry
walked at a distance from the palms and the
shade because he was too young to keep himself out of the sun. He went down the
beach and busied himself at the water's
edge. The great Pacific tide was coming
in and every few seconds the relatively

still water of the lagoon heaved forwards
an inch. There were creatures that lived
in this last fling of the sea, tiny transparencies that came questing in with the
water over the hot, dry sand. With impal-
pable organs of sense they examined this
new field. Perhaps food had appeared
where at the last incursion there had been
none; bird droppings, insects perhaps, any
of the strewn detritus of landward life.
Like a myriad of tiny teeth in a saw, the
transparencies came scavenging over the
beach.

This was fascinating to Henry. He poked
about with a bit of stick, that itself was
wave-worn and whitened and a vagrant, and
tried to control the motions of the scav-
engers. He made little runnels that the
tide filled and tried to crowd them with
creatures. He became absorbed beyond
mere happiness as he felt himself exercising
control over living things. He talked to
them, urging them, ordering them. Driven
back by the tide, his footprints became
bays in which they were trapped and gave
him the illusion of mastery. He squatted
on his hams at the water's edge, bowed, with

a shock of hair falling over his forehead
and past his eyes, and the afternoon sun
emptied down invisible arrows.

Roger waited too. At first he had hidden
behind a great palm; but Henry's absorption
with the transparencies was so obvious
that at last he stood out in full view. He
looked along the beach. Percival had gone
off, crying, and Johnny was left in triumphant possession of the castles. He sat
there, crooning to himself and throwing
sand at an imaginary Percival. Beyond him,
Roger could see the platform and the glints
of spray where Ralph and Simon and Piggy
and Maurice were diving in the pool. He
listened carefully but could only just hear
them.

A sudden breeze shook the fringe of palm
trees, so that the fronds tossed and fluttered. Sixty feet above Roger, several
nuts, fibrous lumps as big as rugby balls,
were loosed from their stems. They fell
about him with a series of hard thumps and
he was not touched. Roger did not con-
sider his escape, but looked from the nuts
to Henry and back again.

The subsoil beneath the palm trees was a
raised beach, and generations of palms had
worked loose in this the stones that had
lain on the sands of another shore. Roger
stopped, picked up a stone, aimed, and
threw it at Henry--threw it to miss. The
stone, that token of preposterous time,
bounced five yards to Henry's right and
fell in the water. Roger gathered a handful of stones and began to throw them. Yet
there was a space round Henry, perhaps six
yards in diameter, into which he dare not
throw. Here, invisible yet strong, was the
taboo of the old life. Round the squatting
child was the protection of parents and
school and policemen and the law. Roger's
arm was conditioned by a civilization that
knew nothing of him and was in ruins.

Henry was surprised by the plopping sounds
in the water. He abandoned the noiseless
transparencies and pointed at the center
of the spreading rings like a setter. This
side and that the stones fell, and Henry
turned obediently but always too late to
see the stones in the air. At last he saw
one and laughed, looking for the friend who
was teasing him. But Roger had whipped

behind the palm again, was leaning against
it breathing quickly, his eyelids fluttering. Then Henry lost interest in stones
and wandered off.

"Roger."

Jack was standing under a tree about ten
yards away. When Roger opened his eyes and
saw him, a darker shadow crept beneath the
swarthiness of his skin; but Jack noticed
nothing. He was eager, impatient, beckon-
ing, so that Roger went to him.

There was a small pool at the end of the
river, dammed back by sand and full of
white water-lilies and needle-like reeds.
Here Sam and Eric were waiting, and Bill.
Jack, concealed from the sun, knelt by the
pool and opened the two large leaves that
he carried. One of them contained white
clay, and the other red. By them lay a
stick of charcoal brought down from the
fire.

Jack explained to Roger as he worked.

"They don't smell me. They see me, I think.
Something pink, under the trees."

He smeared on the clay.

"If only I'd some green!"

He turned a half-concealed face up to Roger
and answered the incomprehension of his
gaze.

"For hunting. Like in the war. You know--
dazzle paint. Like things trying to look
like something else--"

He twisted in the urgency of telling.

"--like moths on a tree trunk."

Roger understood and nodded gravely. The
twins moved toward Jack and began to protest timidly about something. Jack waved
them away.

"Shut up."

He rubbed the charcoal stick between the
patches of red and white on his face.

"No. You two come with me."

He peered at his reflection and disliked it.
He bent down, took up a double handful of

lukewarm water and rubbed the mess from his
face. Freckles and sandy eyebrows appeared.

Roger smiled, unwillingly.

"You don't half look a mess."

Jack planned his new face. He made one
cheek and one eye-socket white, then he
rubbed red over the other half of his face
and slashed a black bar of charcoal across
from right ear to left jaw. He looked in
the pool for his reflection, but his breathing troubled the mirror.

"Samneric. Get me a coconut. An empty
one."

He knelt, holding the shell of water. A
rounded patch of sunlight fell on his face
and a brightness appeared in the depths of
the water. He looked in astonishment, no
longer at himself but at an awesome stran-
ger. He spilt the water and leapt to his
feet, laughing excitedly. Beside the pool
his sinewy body held up a mask that drew
their eyes and appalled them. He began to
dance and his laughter became a bloodthirsty

snarling. He capered toward Bill, and the
mask was a thing on its own, behind which
Jack hid, liberated from shame and self-
consciousness. The face of red and white
and black swung through the air and jigged
toward Bill. Bill started up laughing;
then suddenly he fell silent and blundered
away through the bushes.

Jack rushed toward the twins.

"The rest are making a line. Come on!"

"But--"

"--we--"

"Come on! I'll creep up and stab--"

The mask compelled them.

Ralph climbed out of the bathing pool and
trotted up the beach and sat in the shade
beneath the palms. His fair hair was
plastered over his eyebrows and he pushed
it back. Simon was floating in the water
and kicking with his feet, and Maurice was

practicing diving. Piggy was mooning about, aimlessly picking up things and discarding them. The rock-pools which so fascinated him were covered by the tide, so he was without an interest until the tide went back. Presently, seeing Ralph under the palms, he came and sat by him.

Piggy wore the remainders of a pair of shorts, his fat body was golden brown, and the glasses still flashed when he looked at anything. He was the only boy on the island whose hair never seemed to grow. The rest were shockheaded, but Piggy's hair still lay in wisps over his head as though baldness were his natural state and this imperfect covering would soon go, like the velvet on a young stag's antlers.

"I've been thinking," he said, "about a clock. We could make a sundial. We could put a stick in the sand, and then--"

The effort to express the mathematical processes involved was too great. He made a few passes instead.

"And an airplane, and a TV set," said Ralph sourly, "and a steam engine."

Piggy shook his head.

"You have to have a lot of metal things for
that," he said, "and we haven't got no
metal. But we got a stick."

Ralph turned and smiled involuntarily.
Piggy was a bore; his fat, his ass-mar and
his matter-of-fact ideas were dull, but
there was always a little pleasure to be
got out of pulling his leg, even if one did
it by accident.

Piggy saw the smile and misinterpreted it
as friendliness. There had grown up
tacitly among the biguns the opinion that
Piggy was an outsider, not only by accent,
which did not matter, but by fat, and ass-
mar, and specs, and a certain disinclination
for manual labor. Now, finding that something he had said made Ralph smile, he re-
joiced and pressed his advantage.

"We got a lot of sticks. We could have a
sundial each. Then we should know what the
time was."

"A fat lot of good that would be."

"You said you wanted things done. So as we could be rescued."

"Oh, shut up."

He leapt to his feet and trotted back to the pool, just as Maurice did a rather poor dive. Ralph was glad of a chance to change the subject. He shouted as Maurice came to the surface.

"Belly flop! Belly flop!"

Maurice flashed a smile at Ralph who slid easily into the water. Of all the boys, he was the most at home there; but today, irked by the mention of rescue, the useless, footling mention of rescue, even the green depths of water and the shattered, golden sun held no balm. Instead of remaining and playing, he swam with steady strokes under Simon and crawled out of the other side of the pool to lie there, sleek and streaming like a seal. Piggy, always clum-sy, stood up and came to stand by him, so that Ralph rolled on his stomach and pre-tended not to see. The mirages had died away and gloomily he ran his eye along the taut blue line of the horizon.

The next moment he was on his feet and
shouting.

"Smoke! Smoke!"

Simon tried to sit up in the water and got
a mouthful. Maurice, who had been standing
ready to dive, swayed back on his heels,
made a bolt for the platform, then swerved
back to the grass under the palms. There
he started to pull on his tattered shorts,
to be ready for anything.

Ralph stood, one hand holding back his hair,
the other clenched. Simon was climbing out
of the water. Piggy was rubbing his glasses
on his shorts and squinting at the sea.
Maurice had got both legs through one leg
of his shorts. Of all the boys, only Ralph
was still.

"I can't see no smoke," said Piggy incred-
ulously. "I can't see no smoke, Ralph--
where is it?"

Ralph said nothing. Now both his hands
were clenched over his forehead so that the
fair hair was kept out of his eyes. He was

leaning forward and already the salt was
whitening his body.

"Ralph--where's the ship?"

Simon stood by, looking from Ralph to the
horizon. Maurice's trousers gave way with
a sigh and he abandoned them as a wreck,
rushed toward the forest, and then came
back again.

The smoke was a tight little knot on the
horizon and was uncoiling slowly. Beneath
the smoke was a dot that might be a funnel.
Ralph's face was pale as he spoke to himself.

"They'll see our smoke."

Piggy was looking in the right direction
now.

"It don't look much."

He turned round and peered up at the mountain. Ralph continued to watch the ship,
ravenously. Color was coming back into his
face. Simon stood by him, silent.

"I know I can't see very much," said Piggy, "but have we got any smoke?"

Ralph moved impatiently, still watching the ship.

"The smoke on the mountain."

Maurice came running, and stared out to sea. Both Simon and Piggy were looking up at the mountain. Piggy screwed up his face but Simon cried out as though he had hurt himself.

"Ralph! Ralph!"

The quality of his speech twisted Ralph on the sand.

"You tell me," said Piggy anxiously. "Is there a signal?"

Ralph looked back at the dispersing smoke on the horizon, then up at the mountain.

"Ralph--please! Is there a signal?"

Simon put out his hand, timidly, to touch

Ralph; but Ralph started to run, splashing through the shallow end of the bathing pool, across the hot, white sand and under the palms. A moment later he was battling with the complex undergrowth that was already engulfing the scar. Simon ran after him, then Maurice. Piggy shouted.

"Ralph! Please--Ralph!"

Then he too started to run, stumbling over Maurice's discarded shorts before he was across the terrace. Behind the four boys, the smoke moved gently along the horizon; and on the beach, Henry and Johnny were throwing sand at Percival who was crying quietly again; and all three were in complete ignorance of the excitement.

By the time Ralph had reached the landward end of the scar he was using precious breath to swear. He did desperate violence to his naked body among the rasping creepers so that blood was sliding over him. Just where the steep ascent of the mountain began, he stopped. Maurice was only a few yards behind him.

"Piggy's specs!" shouted Ralph. "If the
fire's all out, we'll need them--"

He stopped shouting and swayed on his feet.
Piggy was only just visible, bumbling up
from the beach. Ralph looked at the horizon, then up to the mountain. Was it better
to fetch Piggy's glasses, or would the ship
have gone? Or if they climbed on, supposing
the fire was all out, and they had to watch
Piggy crawling nearer and the ship sinking
under the horizon? Balanced on a high peak
of need, agonized by indecision, Ralph cried
out:

"Oh God, oh God!"

Simon, struggling with bushes, caught his
breath. His face was twisted. Ralph blundered on, savaging himself, as the wisp of
smoke moved on.

The fire was dead. They saw that straight
away; saw what they had really known down
on the beach when the smoke of home had
beckoned. The fire was out, smokeless and
dead; the watchers were gone. A pile of
unused fuel lay ready.

Ralph turned to the sea. The horizon
stretched, impersonal once more, barren of
all but the faintest trace of smoke. Ralph
ran stumbling along the rocks, saved himself on the edge of the pink cliff, and
screamed at the ship.

"Come back! Come back!"

Simon and Maurice arrived. Ralph looked at
them with unwinking eyes. Simon turned
away, smearing the water from his cheeks.
Ralph reached inside himself for the worst
word he knew.

"They let the bloody fire go out."

He looked down the unfriendly side of the
mountain. Piggy arrived, out of breath and
whimpering like a littlun. Ralph clenched
his fist and went very red. The intentness
of his gaze, the bitterness of his voice,
pointed for him.

"There they are."

A procession had appeared, far down among
the pink stones that lay near the water's

edge.   Some of the boys wore black caps but
otherwise they were almost naked.   They
lifted sticks in the air together whenever
they came to an easy patch.   They were
chanting, something to do with the bundle
that the errant twins carred so carefully.
Ralph picked out Jack easily, even at that
distance, tall, red-haired, and inevitably
leading the procession.

Simon looked now, from Ralph to Jack, as
he had looked from Ralph to the horizon, and
what he saw seemed to make him afraid.
Ralph said nothing more, but waited while
the procession came nearer.   The chant was
audible but at that distance still wordless.
Behind Jack walked the twins, carrying a
great stake on their shoulders.   The gutted
carcass of a pig swung from the stake,
swinging heavily as the twins toiled over
the uneven ground.   The pig's head hung
down with gaping neck and seemed to search
for something on the ground.   At last the
words of the chant floated up to them,
across the bowl of blackened wood and ashes.

"<u>Kill the pig.   Cut her throat.   Spill her
blood</u>."

Yet as the words became audible, the procession reached the steepest part of the
mountain, and in a minute or two the chant
had died away. Piggy sniveled and Simon
shushed him quickly as though he had spoken
too loudly in church.

Jack, his face smeared with clays, reached
the top first and hailed Ralph excitedly,
with lifted spear.

"Look! We've killed a pig--we stole up on
them--we got in a circle--"

Voices broke in from the hunters.

"We got in a circle--"

"We crept up--"

"The pig squealed--"

The twins stood with the pig swinging between them, dropping black gouts on the
rock. They seemed to share one wide,
ecstatic grin. Jack had too many things
to tell Ralph at once. Instead, he danced
a step or two, then remembered his dignity
and stood still, grinning. He noticed

blood on his hands and grimaced distaste-
fully, looked for something on which to
clean them, then wiped them on his shorts
and laughed.

Ralph spoke.

"You let the fire go out."

Jack checked, vaguely irritated by this
irrelevance but too happy to let it worry
him.

"We can light the fire again. You should
have been with us, Ralph. We had a smashing
time. The twins got knocked over--"

"We hit the pig--"

"--I fell on top--"

"I cut the pig's throat," said Jack,
proudly, and yet twitched as he said it.
"Can I borrow yours, Ralph, to make a nick
in the hilt?"

The boys chattered and danced. The twins
continued to grin.

"There was lashings of blood," said Jack, laughing and shuddering, "you should have seen it!"

"We'll go hunting every day--"

Ralph spoke again, hoarsely. He had not moved.

"You let the fire go out."

This repetion made Jack uneasy. He looked at the twins and then back at Ralph.

"We had to have them in the hunt," he said, "or there wouldn't have been enough for a ring."

He flushed, conscious of a fault.

"The fire's only been out an hour or two. We can light up again--"

He noticed Ralph's scarred nakedness, and the sombre silence of all four of them. He sought, charitable in his happiness, to include them in the thing that had happened. His mind was crowded with memories; memories of the knowledge that had come to them when

they closed in on the struggling pig,
knowledge that they had outwitted a living
thing, imposed their will upon it, taken
away its life like a long satisfying drink.

He spread his arms wide.

"You should have seen the blood!"

The hunters were more silent now, but at
this they buzzed again. Ralph flung back
his hair. One arm pointed at the empty
horizon. His voice was loud and savage,
and struck them into silence.

"There was a ship."

Jack, faced at once with too many awful
implications, ducked away from them. He
laid a hand on the pig and drew his knife.
Ralph brought his arm down, fist clenched,
and his voice shook.

"There was a ship. Out there. You said
you'd keep the fire going and you let it
out!" He took a step toward Jack, who
turned and faced him.

"They might have seen us. We might have
gone home--"

This was too bitter for Piggy, who forgot
his timidity in the agony of his loss. He
began to cry out, shrilly:

"You and your blood, Jack Merridew! You
and your hunting! We might have gone
home--"

Ralph pushed Piggy to one side.

"I was chief, and you were going to do what
I said. You talk. But you can't even build
huts--then you go off hunting and let out
the fire--"

He turned away, silent for a moment. Then
his voice came again on a peak of feeling.

"There was a ship--"

One of the smaller hunters began to wail.
The dismal truth was filtering through to
everybody. Jack went very red as he hacked
and pulled at the pig.

"The job was too much. We needed everyone."

Ralph turned.

"You could have had everyone when the shelters were finished. But you had to hunt--"

"We needed meat."

Jack stood up as he said this, the bloodied knife in his hand. The two boys faced each other. There was the brilliant world of hunting, tactics, fierce exhilaration, skill; and there was the world of longing and baffled common-sense. Jack transferred the knife to his left hand and smudged blood over his forehead as he pushed down the plastered hair.

Piggy began again.

"You didn't ought to have let that fire out. You said you'd keep the smoke going--"

This from Piggy, and the wails of agreement from some of the hunters, drove Jack to violence. The bolting look came into his blue eyes. He took a step, and able at last to hit someone, stuck his fist into

Piggy's stomach. Piggy sat down with a
grunt. Jack stood over him. His voice was
vicious with humiliation.

"You would, would you? Fatty!"

Ralph made a step forward and Jack smacked
Piggy's head. Piggy's glasses flew off and
tinkled on the rocks. Piggy cried out in
terror:

"My specs!"

He went crouching and feeling over the
rocks but Simon, who got there first, found
them for him. Passions beat about Simon
on the mountain-top with awful wings.

"One side's broken."

Piggy grabbed and put on the glasses. He
looked malevolently at Jack.

"I got to have them specs. Now I only got
one eye. Jus' you wait--"

Jack made a move toward Piggy who scrambled
away till a great rock lay between them. He

thrust his head over the top and glared at
Jack through his one flashing glass.

"Now I only got one eye. Just you wait--"

Jack mimicked the whine and scramble.

"Jus' you wait--yah!"

Piggy and the parody were so funny that the
hunters began to laugh. Jack felt en-
couraged. He went on scrambling and the
laughter rose to a gale of hysteria. Unwillingly Ralph felt his lips twitch; he
was angry with himself for giving way.

He muttered.

"That was a dirty trick."

Jack broke out of his gyration and stood
facing Ralph. His words came in a shout.

"All right, all right!"

He looked at Piggy, at the hunters, at
Ralph.

"I'm sorry. About the fire, I mean. There.
I--"

He drew himself up.

"--I apologize."

The buzz from the hunters was one of admiration at the handsome behavior. Clearly
they were of the opinion that Jack had done
the decent thing, had put himself in the
right by his generous apology and Ralph,
obscurely, in the wrong. They waited for
an appropriately decent answer.

Yet Ralph's throat refused to pass one. He
resented, as an addition to Jack's mis-
behavior, this verbal trick. The fire was
dead, the ship was gone. Could they not
see? Anger instead of decency passed his
throat.

"That was a dirty trick."

They were silent on the mountain-top while
the opaque look appeared in Jack's eyes and
passed away.

Ralph's final word was an ungracious mutter.

"All right. Light the fire."

With some positive action before them, a
little of the tension died. Ralph said no
more, did nothing, stood looking down at
the ashes round his feet. Jack was loud
and active. He gave orders, sang, whistled,
threw remarks at the silent Ralph--remarks
that did not need an answer, and therefore
could not invite a snub; and still Ralph
was silent. No one, not even Jack, would
ask him to move and in the end they had to
build the fire three yards away and in a
place not really as convenient. So Ralph
asserted his chieftainship and could not
have chosen a better way if he had thought
for days. Against this weapon, so indefin-
able and so effective, Jack was powerless
and raged without knowing why. By the
time the pile was built, they were on
different sides of a high barrier.

When they had dealt with the fire another
crisis arose. Jack had no means of lighting
it. Then to his surprise, Ralph went to
Piggy and took the glasses from him. Not
even Ralph knew how a link between him and
Jack had been snapped and fastened else-
where.

"I'll bring 'em back."

"I'll come too."

Piggy stood behind him, islanded in a sea
of meaningless color, while Ralph knelt and
focused the glossy spot. Instantly the
fire was alight Piggy held out his hands
and grabbed the glasses back.

Before these fantastically attractive
flowers of violet and red and yellow, un-
kindness melted away. They became a circle
of boys round a camp fire and even Piggy
and Ralph were half-drawn in. Soon some of
the boys were rushing down the slope for
more wood while Jack hacked the pig. They
tried holding the whole carcass on a stake
over the fire, but the stake burnt more
quickly than the pig roasted. In the end
they skewered bits of meat on branches and
held them in the flames: and even them almost as much boy was roasted as meat.

Ralph's mouth watered. He meant to refuse
meat but his past diet of fruit and nuts,
with an odd crab or fish, gave him too
little resistance. He accepted a piece of
half-raw meat and gnawed it like a wolf.

Piggy spoke, also dribbling.

"Aren't I having none?"

Jack had meant to leave him in doubt, as
an assertion of power; but Piggy by adver-
tising his omission made more cruelty
necessary.

"You didn't hunt."

"No more did Ralph," said Piggy wetly,
"nor Simon." He amplified. "There isn't
more than a ha'porth of meat in a crab."

Ralph stirred uneasily. Simon, sitting between the twins and Piggy, wiped his mouth
and shoved his piece of meat over the rocks
to Piggy, who grabbed it. The twins giggled and Simon lowered his face in shame.

Then Jack leapt to his feet, slashed off
a great hunk of meat, and flung it down at
Simon's feet.

"Eat! Damn you!"

He glared at Simon.

"Take it!"

He spun on his heel, center of a bewildered circle of boys.

"I got you meat!"

Numberless and inexpressible frustrations combined to make his rage elemental and awe-inspiring.

"I painted my face--I stole up. Now you eat--all of you--and I--"

Slowly the silence on the mountain-top deepened till the click of the fire and the soft hiss of roasting meat could be heard clearly. Jack looked round for understanding but found only respect. Ralph stood among the ashes of the signal fire, his hands full of meat, saying nothing.

Then at last Maurice broke the silence. He changed the subject to the only one that could bring the majority of them together.

"Where did you find the pig?"

Roger pointed down the unfriendly side.
"They were there--by the sea."

Jack, recovering, could not bear to have
his story told. He broke in quickly.

"We spread round. I crept, on hand and
knees. The spears fell out because they
hadn't barbs on. The pig ran away and
made an awful noise--"

"It turned back and ran into the circle,
bleeding--"

All the boys were talking at once, relieved
and excited.

"We closed in--"

The first blow had paralyzed its hind
quarters, so the circle could close in and
beat and beat--

"I cut the pig's throat--"

The twins, still sharing their identical
grin, jumped up and ran round each other.
Then the rest joined in, making pig-dying
noises and shouting.

"One for his nob!"

"Give him a fourpenny one!"

Then Maurice pretended to be the pig and
ran squealing into the center, and the
hunters, circling still, pretended to beat
him. As they danced, they sang.

<u>"Kill the pig. Cut her throat. Bash her
in."</u>

Ralph watched them, envious and resentful.
Not till they flagged and the chant died
away, did he speak.

"I'm calling an assembly."

One by one, they halted, and stood watching
him.

"With the conch. I'm calling a meeting even
if we have to go on into the dark. Down on
the platform. When I blow it. Now."

He turned away and walked off, down the
mountain.

CHAPTER FIVE

BEAST FROM WATER

The tide was coming in and there was only
a narrow strip of firm beach between the
water and the white, stumbling stuff near
the palm terrace. Ralph chose the firm
strip as a path because he needed to think,
and only here could he allow his feet to
move without having to watch them. Suddenly, pacing by the water, he was overcome
with astonishment. He found himself understanding the wearisomeness of this life,
where every path was an improvisation and
a considerable part of one's walking life
was spent watching one's feet. He stopped,
facing the strip; and remembering that
first enthusiastic exploration as though
it were part of a brighter childhood, he
smiled jeeringly. He turned then and
walked back toward the platform with the
sun in his face. The time had come for the
assembly and as he walked into the concealing splendors of the sunlight he went carefully over the points of his speech. There
must be no mistake about this assembly, no
chasing imaginary. . . .

He lost himself in a maze of thoughts that
were rendered vague by his lack of words to
express them. Frowning, he tried again.

This meeting must not be fun, but business.

At that he walked faster, aware all at
once of urgency and the declining sun and
a little wind created by his speed that
breathed about his face. This wind pressed
his grey shirt against his chest so that he
noticed--in this new mood of comprehension--
how the folds were stiff like cardboard,
and unpleasant; noticed too how the frayed
edges of his shorts were making an uncom-
fortable, pink area on the front of his
thighs. With a convulsion of the mind,
Ralph discovered dirt and decay, understood
how much he disliked perpetually flicking
the tangled hair out of his eyes, and at
last, when the sun was gone, rolling noisily to rest among dry leaves. At that he
began to trot.

The beach near the bathing pool was dotted
with groups of boys waiting for the assembly. They made way for him silently, conscious of his grim mood and the fault at
the fire.

The place of assembly in which he stood was
roughly a triangle; but irregular and
sketchy, like everything they made. First
there was the log on which he himself sat;
a dead tree that must have been quite ex-
ceptionally big for the platform. Perhaps
one of those legendary storms of the Pacific
had shifted it here. This palm trunk lay
parallel to the beach, so that when Ralph
sat he faced the island but to the boys was
a darkish figure against the shimmer of the
lagoon. The two sides of the triangle of
which the log was base were less evenly
defined. On the right was a log polished
by restless seats along the top, but not
so large as the chief's and not so comfortable. On the left were four small logs,
one of them--the farthest--lamentably
springy. Assembly after assembly had broken
up in laughter when someone had leaned too
far back and the log had whipped and thrown
half a dozen boys backwards into the grass.
Yet now, he saw, no one had had the wit--
not himself nor Jack, nor Piggy--to bring
a stone and wedge the thing. So they would
continue enduring the ill-balanced twister,
because, because. . . . Again he lost himself in deep waters.

Grass was worn away in front of each trunk
but grew tall and untrodden in the center
of the triangle. Then, at the apex, the
grass was thick again because no one sat
there. All round the place of assembly the
grey trunks rose, straight or leaning, and
supported the low roof of leaves. On two
sides was the beach; behind, the lagoon; in
front, the darkness of the island.

Ralph turned to the chief's seat. They had
never had an assembly as late before. That
was why the place looked so different.
Normally the underside of the green roof
was lit by a tangle of golden reflections,
and their faces were lit upside down--
like, thought Ralph, when you hold an elec-
tric torch in your hands. But now the sun
was slanting in at one side, so that the
shadows were where they ought to be.

Again he fell into that strange mood of
speculation that was so foreign to him. If
faces were different when lit from above or
below--what was a face? What was anything?

Ralph moved impatiently. The trouble was,
if you were a chief you had to think, you

had to be wise. And then the occasion
slipped by so that you had to grab at a
decision. This made you think; because
thought was a valuable thing, that got
results. . . .

Only, decided Ralph as he faced the chief's
seat, I can't think. Not like Piggy.

Once more that evening Ralph had to adjust
his values. Piggy could think. He could
go step by step inside that fat head of
his, only Piggy was no chief. But Piggy,
for all his ludicrous body, had brains.
Ralph was a specialist in thought now, and
could recognize thought in another.

The sun in his eyes reminded him how time
was passing, so he took the conch down from
the tree and examined the surface. Exposure
to the air had bleached the yellow and pink
to near-white, and transparency. Ralph
felt a kind of affectionate reverence for
the conch, even though he had fished the
thing out of the lagoon himself. He faced
the place of assembly and put the conch to
his lips.

The others were waiting for this and came
straight away. Those who were aware that a
ship had passed the island while the fire
was out were subdued by the thought of
Ralph's anger; while those, including the
littluns who did not know, were impressed
by the general air of solemnity. The place
of assembly filled quickly; Jack, Simon,
Maurice, most of the hunters, on Ralph's
right; the rest on the left, under the sun.
Piggy came and stood outside the triangle.
This indicated that he wished to listen,
but would not speak; and Piggy intended it
as a gesture of disapproval.

"The thing is: we need an assembly."

No one said anything but the faces turned
to Ralph were intent. He flourished the
conch. He had learnt as a practical business that fundamental statements like this
had to be said at least twice, before
everyone understood them. One had to sit,
attracting all eyes to the conch, and drop
words like heavy round stones among the
little groups that crouched or squatted.
He was searching his mind for simple words
so that even the littluns would understand
what the assembly was about. Later perhaps,

practiced debaters--Jack, Maurice, Piggy--
would use their whole art to twist the
meeting: but now at the beginning the subject of the debate must be laid out clearly.

"We need an assembly. Not for fun. Not
for laughing and falling off the log"--
the group of littluns on the twister giggled
and looked at each other--"not for making
jokes, or for"--he lifted the conch in an
effort to find the compelling word--"for
cleverness. Not for these things. But to
put things straight."

He paused for a moment.

"I've been alone. By myself I went, thinking what's what. I know what we need. An
assembly to put things straight. And first
of all, I'm speaking."

He paused for a moment and automatically
pushed back his hair. Piggy tiptoed to
the triangle, his ineffectual protest made,
and joined the others.

Ralph went on.

"We have lots of assemblies. Everybody

enjoys speaking and being together. We
decide things. But they don't get done.
We were going to have water brought from
the stream and left in those coconut shells
under fresh leaves. So it was, for a few
days. Now there's no water. The shells
are dry. People drink from the river."

There was a murmur of assent.

"Not that there's anything wrong with drink-
ing from the river. I mean I'd sooner have
water from that place--you know, the pool
where the waterfall is--than out of an old
coconut shell. Only we said we'd have the
water brought. And now not. There were
only two full shells there this afternoon."

He licked his lips.

"Then there's huts. Shelters."

The murmur swelled again and died away.

"You mostly sleep in shelters. Tonight,
except for Samneric up by the fire, you'll
all sleep there. Who built the shelters?"

Clamor rose at once. Everyone had built
the shelters. Ralph had to wave the conch
once more.

"Wait a minute! I mean, who built all
three? We all built the first one, four of
us the second one, and me 'n Simon built
the last one over there. That's why it's
so tottery. No. Don't laugh. That shelter
might fall down if the rain comes back.
We'll need those shelters then."

He paused and cleared his throat.

"There's another thing. We chose those
rocks right along beyond the bathing pool
as a lavatory. That was sensible too. The
tide cleans the place up. You littluns know
about that."

There were sniggers here and there and swift
glances.

"Now people seem to use anywhere. Even near
the shelters and the platform. You littluns, when you're getting fruit; if you're
taken short--"

The assembly roared.

"I said if you're taken short you keep away from the fruit. That's dirty."

Laughter rose again.

"I said that's dirty!"

He plucked at his stiff, grey shirt.

"That's really dirty. If you're taken short you go right along the beach to the rocks. See?"

Piggy held out his hands for the conch but Ralph shook his head. This speech was planned, point by point.

"We've all got to use the rocks again. This place is getting dirty." He paused. The assembly, sensing a crisis, was tensely expectant. "And then: about the fire."

Ralph let out his spare breath with a little gasp that was echoed by his audience. Jack started to chip a piece of wood with his knife and whispered something to Robert, who looked away.

"The fire is the most important thing on
the island. How can we ever be rescued
except by luck, if we don't keep a fire
going? Is a fire too much for us to make?"

He flung out an arm.

"Look at us! How many are we? And yet we
can't keep a fire going to make smoke.
Don't you understand? Can't you see we
ought to--ought to die before we let the
fire out?"

There was a self-conscious giggling among
the hunters. Ralph turned on them passionately.

"You hunters! You can laugh! But I tell
you the smoke is more important than the
pig, however often you kill one. Do all
of you see?" He spread his arms wide and
turned to the whole triangle.

"We've got to make smoke up there--or die!"

He paused, feeling for his next point.

"And another thing."

Someone called out.

"Too many things."

There came mutters of agreement. Ralph
overrode them.

"And another thing. We nearly set the whole
island on fire. And we waste time, rolling
rocks, and making little cooking fires. Now
I say this and make it a rule, because I'm
chief. We won't have a fire anywhere but
on the mountain. Ever."

There was a row immediately. Boys stood
up and shouted and Ralph shouted back.

"Because if you want a fire to cook fish
or crab, you can jolly well go up the mountain. That way we'll be certain."

Hands were reaching for the conch in the
light of the setting sun. He held on and
leapt on the trunk.

"All this I meant to say. Now I've said
it. You voted me for chief. Now you do
what I say."

They quieted, slowly, and at last were
seated again. Ralph dropped down and spoke
in his ordinary voice.

"So remember. The rocks for a lavatory.
Keep the fire going and smoke showing as
a signal. Don't take fire from the mountain. Take your food up there."

Jack stood up, scowling in the gloom, and
held out his hands.

"I haven't finished yet."

"But you've talked and talked!"

"I've got the conch."

Jack sat down, grumbling.

"Then the last thing. This is what people
can talk about."

He waited till the platform was very still.

"Things are breaking up. I don't understand
why. We began well; we were happy. And
then--"

He moved the conch gently, looking beyond
them at nothing, remembering the beastie,
the snake, the fire, the talk of fear.

"Then people started getting frightened."

A murmur, almost a moan, rose and passed
away. Jack had stopped whittling. Ralph
went on, abruptly.

"But that's littluns' talk. We'll get that
straight. So the last part, the bit we can
all talk about, is kind of deciding on the
fear."

The hair was creeping into his eyes again.

"We've got to talk about this fear and
decide there's nothing in it. I'm frightened myself, sometimes; only that's non-
sense! Like bogies. Then, when we've
decided, we can start again and be careful
about things like the fire." A picture
of three boys walking along the bright
beach flitted through his mind. "And be
happy."

Ceremonially, Ralph laid the conch on the

trunk beside him as a sign that the speech
was over. What sunlight reached them was
level.

Jack stood up and took the conch.

"So this is a meeting to find out what's
what. I'll tell you what's what. You
littluns started all this, with the fear
talk. Beasts! Where from? Of course we're
frightened sometimes but we put up with
being frightened. Only Ralph says you
scream in the night. What does that mean
but nightmares? Anyway, you don't hunt or
build or help--you're a lot of cry-babies
and sissies. That's what. And as for the
fear--you'll have to put up with that like
the rest of us."

Ralph looked at Jack open-mouthed, but Jack
took no notice.

"The thing is--fear can't hurt you any more
than a dream. There aren't any beasts to
be afraid of on this island." He looked
along the row of whispering littluns.
"Serve you right if something did get you,
you useless lot of cry-babies! But there
is no animal--"

Ralph interrupted him testily.

"What is all this? Who said anything about an animal?"

"You did, the other day. You said they dream and cry out. Now they talk--not only the littluns, but my hunters sometimes-- talk of a thing, a dark thing, a beast, some sort of animal. I've heard. You thought not, didn't you? Now listen. You don't get big animals on small islands. Only pigs. You only get lions and tigers in big countries like Africa and India--"

"And the Zoo--"

"I've got the conch. I'm not talking about the fear. I'm talking about the beast. Be frightened if you like. But as for the beast--"

Jack paused, cradling the conch, and turned to his hunters with their dirty black caps.

"Am I a hunter or am I not?"

They nodded, simply. He was a hunter all right. No one doubted that.

"Well then--I've been all over this island.
By myself. If there were a beast I'd have
seen it. Be frightened because you're like
that--but there is no beast in the forest."

Jack handed back the conch and sat down.
The whole assembly applauded him with re-
lief. Then Piggy held out his hand.

"I don't agree with all Jack said, but with
some. 'Course there isn't a beast in the
forest. How could there be? What would a
beast eat?"

"Pig."

"We eat pig."

"Piggy!"

"I got the conch!" said Piggy indignantly.
"Ralph--they ought to shut up, oughtn't
they? You shut up, you littluns! What I
mean is that I don't agree about this here
fear. Of course there isn't nothing to be
afraid of in the forest. Why--I been there
myself! You'll be talking about ghosts
and such things next. We know what goes

on and if there's something wrong, there's
someone to put it right."

He took off his glasses and blinked at them.
The sun had gone as if the light had been
turned off.

He proceeded to explain.

"If you get a pain in your stomach, whether
it's a little or a big one--"

"Yours is a big one."

"When you done laughing perhaps we can get
on with the meeting. And if them littluns
climb back on the twister again they'll
only fall of in a sec. So they might as
well sit on the ground and listen. No.
You have doctors for everything, even the
inside of your mind. You don't really mean
that we got to be frightened all the time
of nothing?   Life," said Piggy expansively,
"is scientific, that's what it is. In a
year or two when the war's over they'll be
traveling to Mars and back. I know there
isn't no beast--not with claws and all that,
I mean--but I know there isn't no fear,
either."

Piggy paused.

"Unless--"

Ralph moved restlessly.

"Unless what?"

"Unless we get frightened of people."

A sound, half-laugh, half-jeer, rose among
the seated boys. Piggy ducked his head and
went on hastily.

"So let's hear from that littlun who talked
about a beast and perhaps we can show him
how silly he is."

The littluns began to jabber among themselves, then one stood forward.

"What's your name?"

"Phil."

For a littlun he was self-confident, holding
out his hands, cradling the conch as Ralph
did, looking round at them to collect their
attention before he spoke.

"Last night I had a dream, a horrid dream, fighting with things. I was outside the shelter by myself, fighting with things, those twisty things in the trees."

He paused, and the other littluns laughed in horrified sympathy.

"Then I was frightened and I woke up. And I was outside the shelter by myself in the dark and the twisty things had gone away."

The vivid horror of this, so possible and so nakedly terrifying, held them all silent. The child's voice went piping on from behind the white conch.

"And I was frightened and started to call out for Ralph and then I saw something moving among the trees, something big and horrid."

He paused, half-frightened by the recollection yet proud of the sensation he was creating.

"That was a nightmare," said Ralph. "He was walking in his sleep."

The assembly murmured in subdued agreement.

The littlun shook his head stubbornly.

"I was asleep when the twisty things were fighting and when they went away I was awake, and I saw something big and horrid moving in the trees."

Ralph held out his hands for the conch and the littlun sat down.

"You were asleep. There wasn't anyone there. How could anyone be wandering about in the forest at night? Was anyone? Did anyone go out?"

There was a long pause while the assembly grinned at the thought of anyone going out in the darkness. Then Simon stood up and Ralph looked at him in astonishment.

"You! What were you mucking about in the dark for?"

Simon grabbed the conch convulsively.

"I wanted--to go to a place--a place I know."

"What place?"

"Just a place I know. A place in the jungle."

He hesitated.

Jack settled the question for them with that
contempt in his voice that could sound so
funny and so final.

"He was taken short."

With a feeling of humiliation on Simon's
behalf, Ralph took back the conch, looking
Simon sternly in the face as he did so.

"Well, don't do it again. Understand? Not
at night. There's enough silly talk about
beasts, without the littluns seeing you
gliding about like a--"

The derisive laughter that rose had fear in
it and condemnation. Simon opened his mouth
to speak but Ralph had the conch, so he
backed to his seat.

When the assembly was silent Ralph turned
to Piggy.

"Well, Piggy?"

"There was another one. Him."

The littluns pushed Percival forward, then
left him by himself. He stood knee-deep in
the central grass, looking at his hidden
feet, trying to pretend he was in a tent.
Ralph remembered another small boy who had
stood like this and he flinched away from
the memory. He had pushed the thought down
and out of sight, where only some positive
reminder like this could bring it to the
surface. There had been no further number-
ings of the littluns, partly because
there was no means of insuring that all of
them were accounted for and partly because
Ralph knew the answer to at least one
question Piggy had asked on the mountain-
top. There were little boys, fair, dark,
freckled, and all dirty, but their faces
were all dreadfully free of major blem-
ishes. No one had seen the mulberry-
colored birthmark again. But that time
Piggy had coaxed and bullied. Tacitly
admitting that he remembered the unmention-
able, Ralph nodded to Piggy.

"Go on. Ask him."

Piggy knelt, holding the conch.

"Now then. What's your name?"

The small boy twisted away into his tent.
Piggy turned helplessly to Ralph, who spoke
sharply.

"What's your name?"

Tormented by the silence and the refusal
the assembly broke into a chant.

"What's your name? What's your name?"

"Quiet!"

Ralph peered at the child in the twilight.

"Now tell us. What's your name?"

"Percival Wemys Madison, The Viscarage,
Harcourt St. Anthony, Hants, telephone,
telephone, tele--"

As if this information was rooted far down
in the springs of sorrow, the littlun wept.
His face puckered, the tears leapt from his

eyes, his mouth opened till they could see
a square black hole. At first he was a
silent effigy of sorrow; but then the
lamentation rose out of him, loud and sus-
tained as the conch.

"Shut up, you! Shut up!"

Percival Wemys Madison would not shut up.
A spring had been tapped, far beyond the
reach of authority or even physical intimi-
dation. The crying went on, breath after
breath, and seemed to sustain him upright
as if he were nailed to it.

"Shut up! Shut up!"

For now the littluns were no longer silent.
They were reminded of their personal sor-
rows; and perhaps felt themselves to share
in a sorrow that was universal. They began
to cry in sympathy, two of them almost as
loud as Percival.

Maurice saved them. He cried out.

"Look at me!"

He pretended to fall over. He rubbed his
rump and sat on the twister so that he fell
in the grass. He clowned badly; but
Percival and the others noticed and sniffed
and laughed. Presently they were all
laughing so absurdly that the biguns joined
in.

Jack was the first to make himself heard.
He had not got the conch and thus spoke
against the rules; but nobody minded.

"And what about the beast?"

Something strange was happening to Percival.
He yawned and staggered, so that Jack seized
and shook him.

"Where does the beast live?"

Percival sagged in Jack's grip.

"That's a clever beast," said Piggy, jeer-
ing, "if it can hide on this island."

"Jack's been everywhere--"

"Where could a beast live?"

"Beast my foot!"

Percival muttered something and the assembly
laughed again. Ralph leaned forward.

"What does he say?"

Jack listened to Percival's answer and then
let go of him. Percival, released, surrounded by the comfortable presence of humans, fell in the long grass and went to
sleep.

Jack cleared his throat, then reported
casually.

"He says the beast comes out of the sea."

The last laugh died away. Ralph turned
involuntarily, a black, humped figure
against the lagoon. The assembly looked
with him, considered the vast stretches of
water, the high sea beyond, unknown indigo
of infinite possibility, heard silently
the sough and whisper from the reef.

Maurice spoke, so loudly that they jumped.

"Daddy said they haven't found all the
animals in the sea yet."

Argument started again. Ralph held out the
glimmering conch and Maurice took it obediently. The meeting subsided.

"I mean when Jack says you can be frightened
because people are frightened anyway that's
all right. But when he says there's only
pigs on this island I expect he's right but
he doesn't know, not really, not certainly
I mean--" Maurice took a breath. "My daddy
says there's things, what d'you call'em
that make ink--squids--that are hundreds of
yards long and eat whales whole." He paused
again and laughed gaily. "I don't believe
in the beast of course. As Piggy says,
life's scientific, but we don't know, do
we? Not certainly, I mean--"

Someone shouted.

"A squid couldn't come up out of the water!"

"Could!"

"Couldn't!"

In a moment the platform was full of argu-
ing, gesticulating shadows. To Ralph,
seated, this seemed the breaking up of
sanity. Fear, beasts, no general agreement
that the fire was all-important: and when
one tried to get the thing straight the
argument sheered off, bringing up fresh,
unpleasant matter.

He could see a whiteness in the gloom near
him so he grabbed it from Maurice and blew
as loudly as he could. The assembly was
shocked into silence. Simon was close to
him, laying hands on the conch. Simon felt
a perilous necessity to speak; but to speak
in assembly was a terrible thing to him.

"Maybe," he said hesitantly, "maybe there
is a beast."

The assembly cried out savagely and Ralph
stood up in amazement.

"You, Simon? You believe in this?"

"I don't know," said Simon. His heartbeats
were choking him. "But. . . ."

The storm broke.

"Sit down!"

"Shut up!"

"Take the conch!"

"Sod you!"

"Shut up!"

Ralph shouted.

"Hear him! He's got the conch!"

"What I mean is . . . maybe it's only us."

"Nuts!"

That was from Piggy, shocked out of decorum.
Simon went on.

"We could be sort of. . . ."

Simon became inarticulate in his effort to
express mankind's essential illness. In-
spiration came to him.

"What's the dirtiest thing there is?"

As an answer Jack dropped into the uncom-
prehending silence that followed it the one
crude expressive syllable. Release was
immense. Those littluns who had climbed
back on the twister fell off again and did
not mind. The hunters were screaming with
delight.

Simon's effort fell about him in ruins; the
laughter beat him cruelly and he shrank
away defenseless to his seat.

At last the assembly was silent again.
Someone spoke out of turn.

"Maybe he means it's some sort of ghost."

Ralph lifted the conch and peered into the
gloom. The lightest thing was the pale
beach. Surely the littluns were nearer?
Yes--there was no doubt about it, they were
huddled into a tight knot of bodies in the
central grass. A flurry of wind made the
palms talk and the noise seemed very loud
now that darkness and silence made it so
noticeable. Two grey trunks rubbed each
other with an evil squeaking that no one
had noticed by day.

Piggy took the conch out of his hands. His
voice was indignant.

"I don't believe in no ghosts--ever!"

Jack was up too, unaccountably angry.

"Who cares what you believe--Fatty!"

"I got the conch!"

There was the sound of a brief tussle and
the conch moved to and fro.

"You gimme the conch back!"

Ralph pushed between them and got a thump
on the chest. He wrested the conch from
someone and sat down breathlessly.

"There's too much talk about ghosts. We
ought to have left all this for daylight."

A hushed and anonymous voice broke in.

"Perhaps that's what the beast is--a ghost."

The assembly was shaken as by a wind.

"There's too much talking out of turn,"
Ralph said, "because we can't have proper
assemblies if you don't stick to the rules."

He stopped again. The careful plan of this
assembly had broken down.

"What d'you want me to say then? I was
wrong to call this assembly so late. We'll
have a vote on them; on ghosts I mean; and
then go to the shelters because we're all
tired. No--Jack is it?--wait a minute.
I'll say here and now that I don't believe
in ghosts. Or I don't think I do. But I
don't like the thought of them. Not now
that is, in the dark. But we were going
to decide what's what."

He raised the conch for a moment.

"Very well then. I suppose what's what is
whether there are ghosts or not--"

He thought for a moment, formulating the
question.

"Who thinks there may be ghosts?"

For a long time there was silence and no

apparent movement. Then Ralph peered into
the gloom and made out the hands. He spoke
flatly.

"I see."

The world, that understandable and lawful
world, was slipping away. Once there was
this and that; and now--and the ship had
gone.

The conch was snatched from his hands and
Piggy's voice shrilled.

"I didn't vote for no ghosts!"

He whirled round on the assembly.

"Remember that, all of you!"

They heard him stamp.

"What are we? Humans? Or animals? Or
savages? What's grownups going to think?
Going off--hunting pigs--letting fires out
--and now!"

A shadow fronted him tempestuously.

"You shut up, you fat slug!"

There was a moment's struggle and the glimmering conch jigged up and down. Ralph
leapt to his feet.

"Jack! Jack! You haven't got the conch!
Let him speak."

Jack's face swam near him.

"And you shut up! Who are you, anyway?
Sitting there telling people what to do.
You can't hunt, you can't sing--"

"I'm chief. I was chosen."

"Why should choosing make any difference?
Just giving orders that don't make any
sense--"

"Piggy's got the conch."

"That's right--favor Piggy as you always
do--"

"Jack!"

Jack's voice sounded in bitter mimicry.

"Jack! Jack!"

"The rules!" shouted Ralph. "You're breaking the rules!"

"Who cares?"

Ralph summoned his wits.

"Because the rules are the only thing we've
got!"

But Jack was shouting against him.

"Bollocks to the rules! We're strong--we
hunt! If there's a beast, we'll hunt it
down! We'll close in and beat and beat and
beat--!"

He gave a wild whoop and leapt down to the
pale sand. At once the platform was full
of noise and excitement, scramblings,
screams and laughter. The assembly shredded
away and became a discursive and random
scatter from the palms to the water and
away along the beach, beyond night-sight.
Ralph found his cheek touching the conch
and took it from Piggy.

"What's grownups going to say?" cried Piggy
again. "Look at 'em!"

The sound of mock hunting, hysterical laughter and real terror came from the beach.

"Blow the conch, Ralph."

Piggy was so close that Ralph could see
the glint of his one glass.

"There's the fire. Can't they see?"

"You got to be tough now. Make 'em do what
you want."

Ralph answered in the cautious voice of one
who rehearses a theorem.

"If I blow the conch and they don't come
back; then we've had it. We shan't keep the
fire going. We'll be like animals. We'll
never be rescued."

"If you don't blow, we'll soon be animals
anyway. I can't see what they're doing
but I can hear."

The dispersed figures had come together on
the sand and were a dense black mass that
revolved. They were chanting something
and littluns that had had enough were
staggering away, howling. Ralph raised
the conch to his lips and then lowered it.

"The trouble is: Are there ghosts, Piggy?
Or beasts?"

"Course there aren't."

"Why not?"

"'Cos things wouldn't make sense. Houses
an' streets, an'--TV--they wouldn't work."

The dancing, chanting boys had worked themselves away till their sound was nothing
but a wordless rhythm.

"But s'pose they don't make sense? Not
here, on this island? Supposing things are
watching us and waiting?"

Ralph shuddered violently and moved closer
to Piggy, so that they bumped frighten-
ingly.

"You stop talking like that! We got enough
trouble, Ralph, an' I've had as much as I
can stand. If there is ghosts--"

"I ought to give up being chief. Hear 'em."

"Oh lord! Oh no!"

Piggy gripped Ralph's arm.

"If Jack was chief he'd have all hunting
and no fire. We'd be here till we died."

His voice ran up to a squeak.

"Who's that sitting there?"

"Me. Simon."

"Fat lot of good we are," said Ralph.
"Three blind mice. I'll give up."

"If you give up," said Piggy, in an appalled
whisper, "what'ud happen to me?"

"Nothing."

"He hates me. I dunno why. If he could do

what he wanted--you're all right, he re-
spects you. Besides--you'd hit him."

"You were having a nice fight with him just
now."

"I had the conch," said Piggy simply. "I
had a right to speak."

Simon stirred in the dark.

"Go on being chief."

"You shut up, young Simon! Why couldn't
you say there wasn't a beast?"

"I'm scared of him," said Piggy, "and that's
why I know him. If you're scared of someone you hate him but you can't stop thinking
about him. You kid yourself he's all right
really, an' then when you see him again;
it's like asthma an' you can't breathe. I
tell you what. He hates you too, Ralph--"

"Me? Why me?"

"I dunno. You got him over the fire; an'
you're chief an' he isn't."

"But he's, he's, Jack Merridew!"

"I been in bed so much I done some thinking.
I know about people. I know about me. And
him. He can't hurt you: but if you stand
out of the way he'd hurt the next thing.
And that's me."

"Piggy's right, Ralph. There's you and
Jack. Go on being chief."

"We're all drifting and things are going
rotten. At home there was always a grownup.
Please, sir; please, miss; and then you got
an answer. How I wish!"

"I wish my auntie was here."

"I wish my father . . . Oh, what's the use?"

"Keep the fire going."

The dance was over and the hunters were
going back to the shelters.

"Grownups know things," said Piggy. "They
ain't afraid of the dark. They'd meet and
have tea and discuss. Then things 'ud be
all right--"

"They wouldn't set fire to the island. Or
lose--"

"They'd build a ship--"

The three boys stood in the darkness, striv-
ing unsuccessfully to convey the majesty
of adult life.

"They wouldn't quarrel--"

"Or break my specs--"

"Or talk about a beast--"

"If only they could get a message to us,"
cried Ralph desperately. "If only they
could send us something grown-up . . . a
sign or something."

A thin wail out of the darkness chilled them
and set them grabbing for each other. Then
the wail rose, remote and unearthly, and
turned to an inarticulate gibbering. Percival Wemys Madison, of the Vicarage, Harcourt St. Anthony, lying in the long grass,
was living through circumstances in which
the incantation of his address was powerless
to help him.

CHAPTER SIX

BEAST FROM AIR

There was no light left save that of the
stars. When they had understood what made
the ghostly noise and Percival was quiet
again, Ralph and Simon picked him up un-
handily and carried him to a shelter. Piggy
hung about near for all his brave words, and
the three bigger boys went together to the
next shelter. They lay restlessly and noisily among the dry leaves, watching the patch
of stars that was the opening toward the lagoon. Sometimes a littlun cried out from
the other shelters and once a bigun spoke
in the dark. Then they too fell asleep.

A sliver of moon rose over the horizon,
hardly large enough to make a path of light
even when it sat right down on the water;
but there were other lights in the sky,
that moved fast, winked, or went out,
though not even a faint popping came down
from the battle fought at ten miles' height.
But a sign came down from the world of
grownups, though at the time there was no
child awake to read it. There was a sudden

bright explosion and a corkscrew trail
across the sky; then darkness again and
stars. There was a speck above the island,
a figure dropping swiftly beneath a parachute, a figure that hung with dangling
limbs. The changing winds of various alti-
tudes took the figure where they would.
Then, three miles up, the wind steadied and
bore it in a descending curve round the sky
and swept it in a great slant across the
reef and the lagoon toward the mountain.
The figure fell and crumpled among the blue
flowers of the mountain-side, but now there
was a gentle breeze at this height too and
the parachute flopped and banged and pulled.
So the figure, with feet that dragged behind
it, slid up the mountain. Yard by yard,
puff by puff, the breeze hauled the figure
through the blue flowers, over the boulders
and red stones, till it lay huddled among
the shattered rocks of the mountain-top.
Here the breeze was fitful and allowed the
strings of the parachute to tangle and
festoon; and the figure sat, its helmeted
head between its knees, held by a complica-
tion of lines. When the breeze blew, the
lines would strain taut and some accident
of this pull lifted the head and chest

upright so that the figure seemed to peer
across the brow of the mountain. Then, each
time the wind dropped, the lines would
slacken and the figure bow forward again,
sinking its head between its knees. So as
the stars moved across the sky, the figure
sat on the mountain-top and bowed and sank
and bowed again.

In the darkness of early morning there were
noises by a rock a little way down the side
of the mountain. Two boys rolled out of
a pile of brushwood and dead leaves, two
dim shadows talking sleepily to each other.
They were the twins, on duty at the fire.
In theory one should have been asleep and
one on watch. But they could never manage
to do things sensibly if that meant acting
independently, and since staying awake all
night was impossible, they had both gone
to sleep. Now they approched the darker
smudge that had been the signal fire, yawning, rubbing their eyes, treading with
practiced feet. When they reached it they
stopped yawning, and one ran quickly back
for brushwood and leaves.

The other knelt down.

"I believe it's out."

He fiddled with the sticks that were pushed into his hands.

"No."

He lay down and put his lips close to the smudge and blew softly. His face appeared, lit redly. He stopped blowing for a moment.

"Sam--give us--"

"--tinder wood."

Eric bent down and blew softly again till the patch was bright. Sam poked the piece of tinder wood into the hot spot, then a branch. The glow increased and the branch took fire. Sam piled on more branches.

"Don't burn the lot," said Eric, "you're putting on too much."

"Let's warm up."

"We'll only have to fetch more wood."

"I'm cold."

"So'm I."

"Besides, it's--"

"--dark. All right, then."

Eric squatted back and watched Sam make up
the fire. He built a little tent of dead
wood and the fire was safely alight.

"That was near."

"He'd have been--"

"Waxy."

"Huh."

For a few moments the twins watched the fire
in silence. Then Eric sniggered.

"Wasn't he waxy?"

"About the--"

"Fire and the pig."

"Lucky he went for Jack, 'stead of us."

"Huh.   Remember old Waxy at school?"

"'Boy--you-are-driving-me-slowly-insane!'"

The twins shared their identical laughter,
then remembered the darkness and other
things and glanced round uneasily. The
flames, busy about the tent, drew their
eyes back again. Eric watched the scurrying
woodlice that were so frantically unable to
avoid the flames, and thought of the first
fire--just down there, on the steeper side
of the mountain, where now was complete
darkness. He did not like to remember it,
and looked away at the mountain-top.

Warmth radiated now, and beat pleasantly
on them. Sam amused himself by fitting
branches into the fire as closely as possible. Eric spread out his hands, searching
for the distance at which the head was just
bearable. Idly looking beyond the fire,
he resettled the scattered rocks from their
flat shadows into daylight contours. Just
there was the big rock, and the three
stones there, that split rock, and there
beyond was a gap--just there--

"Sam."

"Huh?"

"Nothing."

The flames were mastering the branches,
the bark was curling and falling away, the
wood exploding. The tent fell inwards and
flung a wide circle of light over the mountain-top.

"Sam--"

"Huh?"

"Sam!   Sam!"

Sam looked at Eric irritably. The intensity
of Eric's gaze made the direction in which
he looked terrible, for Sam had his back to
it. He scrambled round the fire, squatted
by Eric, and looked to see. They became
motionless, gripped in each other's arms,
four unwinking eyes aimed and two mouths
open.

Far beneath them, the trees of the forest
sighed, then roared. The hair on their
foreheads fluttered and flames blew out

sideways from the fire. Fifteen yards away
from them came the plopping noise of fabric
blown open.

Neither of the boys screamed but the grip
of their arms tightened and their mouths
grew peaked. For perhaps ten seconds they
crouched like that while the flailing fire
sent smoke and sparks and waves of incon-
stant light over the top of the mountain.

Then as though they had but one terrified
mind between them they scrambled away over
the rocks and fled.

Ralph was dreaming. He had fallen asleep
after what seemed hours of tossing and
turning noisily among the dry leaves. Even
the sounds of nightmare from the other
shelters no longer reached him, for he was
back to where he came from, feeding the
ponies with sugar over the garden wall.
Then someone was shaking his arm, telling
him that it was time for tea.

"Ralph! Wake up!"

The leaves were roaring like the sea.

"Ralph, wake up!"

"What's the matter?"

"We saw--"

"--the beast--"

"--plain!"

"Who are you? The twins?"

"We saw the beast--"

"Quiet. Piggy!"

The leaves were roaring still. Piggy bumped into him and a twin grabbed him as he made for the oblong of paling stars.

"You can't go out--it's horrible!"

"Piggy--where are the spears?"

"I can hear the--"

"Quiet then. Lie still."

They lay there listening, at first with
doubt but then with terror to the descrip-
tion the twins breathed at them between
bouts of extreme silence. Soon the darkness
was full of claws, full of the awful unknown
and menace. An interminable dawn faded the
stars out, and at last light, sad and grey,
filtered into the shelter. They began to
stir though still the world outside the
shelter was impossibly dangerous. The maze
of the darkness sorted into near and far,
and at the high point of the sky the cloud-
lets were warmed with color. A single sea
bird flapped upwards with a hoarse cry that
was echoed presently, and something squawked
in the forest. Now streaks of cloud near
the horizon began to glow rosily, and the
feathery tops of the palms were green.

Ralph knelt in the entrance to the shelter
and peered cautiously round him.

"Sam 'n Eric. Call them to assembly. Quietly. Go on."

The twins, holding tremulously to each
other, dared the few yards to the next
shelter and spread the dreadful news. Ralph
stood up and walked for the sake of dignity,

though with his back pricking, to the platform. Piggy and Simon followed him and the other boys came sneaking after.

Ralph took the conch from where it lay on the polished seat and held it to his lips; but then he hesitated and did not blow. He held the shell up instead and showed it to them and they understood.

The rays of the sun that were fanning upwards from below the horizon swung downwards to eye-level. Ralph looked for a moment at the growing slice of gold that lit them from the right hand and seemed to make speech possible. The circle of boys before him bristled with hunting spears.

He handed the conch to Eric, the nearest of the twins.

"We've seen the beast with our own eyes. No--we weren't asleep--"

Sam took up the story, By custom now one conch did for both twins, for their substantial unity was recognized.

"It was furry. There was something moving
behind its head--wings. The beast moved
too--"

"That was awful. It kind of sat up--"

"The fire was bright--"

"We'd just made it up--"

"--more sticks on--"

"There were eyes--"

"Teeth--"

"Claws--"

"We ran as fast as we could--"

"Bashed into things--"

"The beast followed us--"

"I saw it slinking behind the trees--"

"Nearly touched me--"

Ralph pointed fearfully at Eric's face,
which was striped with scars where the
bushes had torn him.

"How did you do that?"

Eric felt his face.

"I'm all rough. Am I bleeding?"

The circle of boys shrank away in horror.
Johnny, yawning still, burst into noisy
tears and was slapped by Bill till he choked
on them. The bright morning was full of
threats and the circle began to change. It
faced out, rather than in, and the spears
of sharpened wood were like a fence. Jack
called them back to center.

"This'll be a real hunt! Who'll come?"

Ralph moved impatiently.

"These spears are made of wood. Don't be
silly."

Jack sneered at him.

"Frightened?"

"'Course I'm frightened. Who wouldn't be?"

He turned to the twins, yearning but hopeless.

"I suppose you aren't pulling our legs?"

The reply was too emphatic for anyone to
doubt them.

Piggy took the conch.

"Couldn't we--kind of--stay here? Maybe
the beast won't come near us."

But for the sense of something watching
them, Ralph would have shouted at him.

"Stay here? And be cramped into this bit
of the island, always on the lookout? How
should we get food? And what about the
fire?"

"Let's be moving," said Jack restlessly,
"we're wasting time."

"No we're not. What about the littluns?"

"Sucks to the littluns!"

"Someone's got to look after them."

"Nobody has so far."

"There was no need! Now there is. Piggy'll look after them."

"That's right. Keep Piggy out of danger."

"Have some sense. What can Piggy do with only one eye?"

The rest of the boys were looking from Jack to Ralph, curiously.

"And another thing. You can't have an ordinary hunt because the beast doesn't leave tracks. If it did you'd have seen them. For all we know, the beast may swing through the trees like what's its name."

They nodded.

"So we've got to think."

Piggy took off his damaged glasses and cleaned the remaining lens.

"How about us, Ralph?"

"You haven't got the conch. Here."

"I mean--how about us? Suppose the beast comes when you're all away. I can't see proper, and if I get scared--"

Jack broke in contemptuously.

"You're always scared."

"I got the conch--"

"Conch! Conch!" shouted Jack. "We don't need the conch any more. We know who ought to say things. What good did Simon do speaking, or Bill, or Walter? It's time some people knew they've got to keep quiet and leave deciding things to the rest of us."

Ralph could no longer ignore his speech. The blood was hot in his cheeks.

"You haven't got the conch," he said. "Sit down."

Jack's face went so white that the freckles showed as clear, brown flecks. He licked his lips and remained standing.

"This is a hunter's job."

The rest of the boys watched intently.
Piggy, finding himself uncomfortably em-
broiled, slid the conch to Ralph's knees
and sat down. The silence grew oppressive
and Piggy held his breath.

"This is more than a hunter's job," said
Ralph at last, "because you can't track
the beast. And don't you want to be
rescued?"

He turned to the assembly.

"Don't you all want to be rescued?"

He looked back at Jack.

"I said before, the fire is the main thing.
Now the fire must be out--"

The old exasperation saved him and gave
him the energy to attack.

"Hasn't anyone got any sense? We've got to
relight that fire. You never thought of
that, Jack, did you? Or don't any of you
want to be rescued?"

Yes, they wanted to be rescued, there was
no doubt about that; and with a violent
swing to Ralph's side, the crisis passed.
Piggy let out his breath with a gasp,
reached for it again and failed. He lay
against a log, his mouth gapping, blue
shadows creeping round his lips. Nobody
minded him.

"Now think, Jack. Is there anywhere on the
island you haven't been?"

Unwillingly Jack answered.

"There's only--but of course! You remember?
The tail-end part, where the rocks are all
piled up. I've been near there. The rock
makes a sort of bridge. There's only one
way up."

"And the thing might live there."

All the assembly talked at once.

"Quiet! All right. That's where we'll
look. If the beast isn't there we'll go
up the mountain and look; and light the
fire."

"Let's go."

"We'll eat first. Then go." Ralph paused.
"We'd better take spears."

After they had eaten, Ralph and the biguns
set out along the beach. They left Piggy
propped up on the platform. This day prom-
ised, like the others, to be a sunbath under
a blue dome. The beach stretched away
before them in a gentle curve till perspec-
tive drew it into one with the forest; for
the day was not advanced enough to be ob-
scured by the shifting veils of mirage.
Under Ralph's direction, they picked a
careful way along the palm terrace, rather
than dare the hot sand down by the water.
He let Jack lead the way; and Jack trod
with theatrical caution though they could
have seen an enemy twenty yards away. Ralph
walked in the rear, thankful to have es-
caped responsibility for a time.

Simon, walking in front of Ralph, felt a
flicker of incredulity--a beast with claws
that scratched, that sat on a mountain-top,
that left no tracks and yet was not fast
enough to catch Samneric. However Simon

thought of the beast, there rose before his inward sight the picture of a human at once heroic and sick.

He sighed. Other people could stand up and speak to an assembly, apparently, without that dreadful feeling of the pressure of personality; could say what they would as though they were speaking to only one person. He stepped aside and looked back. Ralph was coming along, holding his spear over his shoulder. Diffidently, Simon allowed his pace to slacken until he was walking side by side with Ralph and looking up at him through the coarse black hair that now fell to his eyes. Ralph glanced sideways, smiled constrainedly as though he had forgotten that Simon had made a fool of himself, then looked away again at nothing. For a moment or two Simon was happy to be accepted and then he ceased to think about himself. When he bashed into a tree Ralph looked sideways impatiently and Robert sniggered. Simon reeled and a white spot on his forehead turned red and trickled. Ralph dismissed Simon and returned to his personal hell. They would reach the castle some time; and the chief would have to go forward.

Jack came trotting back.

"We're in sight now."

"All right. We'll get as close as we can."

He followed Jack toward the castle where the
ground rose slightly. On their left was an
impenetrable tangle of creepers and trees.

"Why couldn't there be something in that?"

"Because you can see. Nothing goes in or
out."

"What about the castle then?"

Ralph parted the screen of grass and looked
out. There were only a few more yards of
stony ground and then the two sides of the
island came almost together so that one
expected a peak of headland. But instead
of this a narrow ledge of rock, a few yards
wide and perhaps fifteen feet long, continued the island out into the sea. There
lay another of those pieces of pink squareness that underlay the structure of the
island. This side of the castle, perhaps

a hundred feet high, was the pink bastion
they had seen from the mountain-top. The
rock of the cliff was split and the top
littered with great lumps that seemed to
totter.

Behind Ralph the tall grass had filled with
silent hunters. Ralph looked at Jack.

"You're a hunter."

Jack went red.

"I know. All right."

Something deep in Ralph spoke for him.

"I'm chief. I'll go. Don't argue."

He turned to the others.

"You. Hide here. Wait for me."

He found his voice tended either to dis-
appear or to come out too loud. He looked
at Jack.

"Do you--think?"

Jack muttered.

"I've been all over. It must be here."

"I see."

Simon mumbled confusedly: "I don't believe
in the beast."

Ralph answered him politely, as if agreeing
about the weather.

"No. I suppose not."

His mouth was tight and pale. He put back
his hair very slowly.

"Well. So long."

He forced his feet to move until they had
carried him out on to the neck of land.

He was surrounded on all sides by chasms of
empty air. There was nowhere to hide, even
if one did not have to go on. He paused on
the narrow neck and looked down. Soon, in
a matter of centuries, the sea would make
an island of the castle. On the right hand

was the lagoon, troubled by the open sea;
and on the left--

Ralph shuddered. The lagoon had protected
them from the Pacific: and for some reason
only Jack had gone right down to the water
on the other side. Now he saw the lands-
man's view of the swell and it seemed like
the breathing of some stupendous creature.
Slowly the waters sank among the rocks,
revealing pink tables of granite, strange
growths of coral, polyp, and weed. Down,
down, the waters were whispering like the
wind among the heads of the forest. There
was one flat rock there, spread like a
table, and the waters sucking down on the
four weedy sides made them seem like cliffs.
Then the sleeping leviathan breathed out,
the waters rose, the weed streamed, and the
water boiled over the table rock with a
roar. There was no sense of the passage
of waves; only this minute-long fall and
rise and fall.

Ralph turned away to the red cliff. They
were waiting behind him in the long grass,
waiting to see what he would do. He noticed
that the sweat in his palm was cool now;

realized with surprise that he did not
really expect to meet any beast and didn't
know what he would do about it if he did.

He saw that he could climb the cliff but
this was not necessary. The squareness of
the rock allowed a sort of plinth round
it, so that to the right, over the lagoon,
one could inch along a ledge and turn the
corner out of sight. It was easy going, and
soon he was peering round the rock.

Nothing but what you might expect: pink,
tumbled boulders with guano layered on them
like icing; and a steep slope up to the
shattered rocks that crowned the bastion.

A sound behind him made him turn. Jack was
edging along the ledge.

"Couldn't let you do it on your own."

Ralph said nothing. He led the way over
the rocks, inspected a sort of half-cave
that held nothing more terrible than a
clutch of rotten eggs, and at last sat down,
looking round him and tapping the rock with
the butt of his spear.

Jack was excited.

"What a place for a fort!"

A column of spray wetted them.

"No fresh water."

"What's that then?"

There was indeed a long green smudge half-
way up the rock. They climbed up and
tasted the trickle of water.

"You could keep a coconut shell there,
filling all the time.

"Not me. This is a rotten place."

Side by side they scaled the last height
to where the diminishing pile was crowned
by the last broken rock. Jack struck the
near one with his fist and it grated
slightly.

"Do you remember--?"

Consciousness of the bad times in between
came to them both. Jack talked quickly.

"Shove a palm trunk under that and if an
enemy came--look!"

A hundred feet below them was the narrow
causeway, then the stony ground, then the
grass dotted with heads, and behind that
the forest.

"One heave," cried Jack, exulting, "and--
wheee--!"

He made a sweeping movement with his hand.
Ralph looked toward the mountain.

"What's the matter?"

Ralph turned.

"Why?"

"You were looking--I don't know why."

"There's no signal now. Nothing to show."

"You're nuts on the signal."

The taut blue horizon encircled them,
broken only by the mountain top.

"That's all we've got."

He leaned his spear against the rocking stone and pushed back two handfuls of hair.

"We'll have to go back and climb the mountain. That's where they saw the beast.

"The beast won't be there."

"What else can we do?"

The others, waiting in the grass, saw Jack and Ralph unharmed and broke cover into the sunlight. They forgot the beast in the excitement of exploration. They swarmed across the bridge and soon were climbing and shouting. Ralph stood now, one hand against an enormous red block, a block large as a mill wheel that had been split off and hung, tottering. Somberly he watched the mountain. He clenched his fist and beat hammer-wise on the red wall at his right. His lips were tightly compressed and his eyes yearned beneath the frings of hair.

"Smoke."

He sucked his bruised fist.

"Jack!   Come on."

But Jack was not there. A knot of boys,
making a great noise that he had not noticed, were heaving and pushing at a rock.
As he turned, the base cracked and the whole
mass toppled into the sea so that a thunder-
ous plume of spray leapt half-way up the
cliff.

"Stop it!   Stop it!"

His voice struck a silence among them.

"Smoke."

A strange thing happened to his head. Something flittered there in front of his mind
like a bat's wing, obscuring his idea.

"Smoke."

At once the ideas were back, and the anger.

"We want smoke. And you go wasting your
time. You roll rocks."

Roger shouted.

"We've got plenty of time!"

Ralph shook his head.

"We'll go to the mountain."

The clamor broke out. Some of the boys wanted to go back to the beach. Some wanted to roll more rocks. The sun was bright and danger had faded with the darkness.

"Jack. The beast might be on the other side. You can lead again. You've been."

"We could go by the shore. There's fruit."

Bill came up to Ralph.

"Why can't we stay here for a bit?"

"That's right."

"Let's have a fort."

"There's no food here," said Ralph, "and no shelter. Not much fresh water."

"This would make a wizard fort."

"We can roll rocks--"

"Right onto the bridge--"

"I say we'll go on!" shouted Ralph furi-
ously. "We've got to make certain. We'll
go now."

"Let's stay here--"

"Back to the shelter--"

"I'm tired--"

"No!"

Ralph struck the skin off his knuckles.
They did not seem to hurt.

"I'm chief. We've got to make certain.
Can't you see the mountain? There's no
signal showing. There may be a ship out
there. Are you all off your rockers?"

Mutinously, the boys fell silent or muttering.

Jack led the way down the rock and across
the bridge.